A MATTER OF HONOR

Con Flannery raised his rough voice to a full-throated roar. "Listen to me, you storekeepers and moneygrubbers, and listen good! There's been talk around about my daughter. Gutter talk—you all know what you've been saying. There's talk about my daughter and a low, sneaking, bloody-handed son of a bitch with the name Ballard. Dirty men have come here to spread dirty money to see that she goes back to this man. You all think you're going to get rich with more dirty money if she does. But I'm here to tell you that if this talk goes on, a lot of you are going to get killed. And that, you half-men, is a promise."

Other Leisure Books in the *Saddler* series:

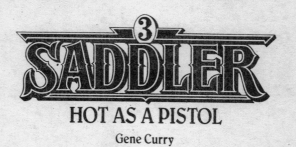

SADDLER 3

HOT AS A PISTOL

Gene Curry

LEISURE BOOKS   NEW YORK CITY

A LEISURE BOOK®

December 1990

Published by

Dorchester Publishing Co., Inc.
276 Fifth Avenue
New York, NY 10001

Printed in the United States of America.

ONE

Women have a way of getting me into trouble, but I give them a lot of help. This time though it was a fellow Texan who set me on the road to ruin. They called him Gentleman Johnny Callahan and we both came from the same part of West Texas, me from Jonesboro, Callahan from Dimmit. I had known Johnny most of my life, and while both of us had been raised by the ears, as they say in the Panhandle, I never brooded about it. My folks were poor but all right in their way, doing what they could for the kids. So being poor didn't bother me the way it did Callahan.

Years back, I remember him saying he would never, never again wear old clothes, any kind of hand-me-downs—no more patched overalls and broken boots for Johnny. He was going to dress like a gent, and he did, right from the day he got his first handful of folding money. I lost track of him for a few years; then I began to hear about him, mostly in Texas. After some false starts—running wet cows into Mexico, the finding of "stray" horses, and the like—old Johnny became a town tamer, a pacifier of little hellholes all over Texas. Not that John Callahan was a killer; he'd much rather cheat a man at cards than kill him. Naturally, in the line of work he followed, he had to douse the lamps of a few badmen, but backshooting and shotgunning wasn't much to his liking. Like I say, he did it for a living.

It went along like that for a while. I ran into him a few times, and while you'd have to stretch it to the breaking point to call us bosom pals, we got along well enough, things considering. We came from the hard part of Texas and away from there any kind of friendship counted for something.

The funny thing was that Johnny made a small but solid rep for himself, and then just dropped out of sight. He was seen no more in the fleshpots of Fort Griffin; they missed his nervy playing in the poker games of El Paso. After a few years, people began to say he was dead. There were more than a few daring liars who had seen him die, had witnessed his demise at the hands of any number of notorious desperados. Only one thing was sure, Gentleman Johnny Callahan was gone.

The last place I expected to find him was in the town of Dragoon Wells, in the Arizona Territory. I knew there was a town of that name three or four days ride from the Sonora border. Back in the '60's when the Apaches were running wild, with most of the men off to fight in Abe Lincoln's war, a few old codgers who had been dragoons in Alamo times stood off a whole mess of Indians and saved the town. Hence the name. All that stuff I learned later after I got to be marshal of the town.

I was on my way south to see what Mexico had to offer in the way of easy money. Dragoon Wells was on the way. Things happened and I stayed over and got into trouble.

I rode into town on a Sunday afternoon, and out on the edge of this benighted place some of the sports had a horse race going. On the bare brown hills surrounding the town were worked-out mines, the galvanized-iron sheeting of the buildings rusting in the sun. A second growth of brush was doing its best to cover the scarred hillsides. The sky was bright and clear, and it was hot. It didn't look like much of a town.

I was in no special hurry—my intention was to bunk in for the night, start again come morning—so I hung around for the races. I didn't get a good look at Johnny Callahan until he fell off the horse. That was right at the finish of the race. They were heading for the finish line and the rider who turned out to be Johnny was far in the lead, whacking his coal-black Arabian with his hat, urging the spirited critter to greater speed. There was no need to put all that distance between himself and the losers, but then Johnny always was a show-off.

That Arabian had his tail out straight as a poker and if he'd gone any faster he'd have been flying. He hit the finish ribbon like a bolt of lightning, and then it happened. Right at that instant some dog decided to commit suicide by running right under the Arabian. The dog got killed and the rider got thrown, as if pitched from one of those Roman catapults. He had a short, graceful flight and came down heavy. So heavy and hard you could hear his legs breaking above the groan that went up from the crowd. A few people stared at me as I drifted along to see the damage, but the main attraction was the bunged-up rider. He lay there cursing a blue streak, and when I got a better look I saw old Johnny Callahan.

I guess he was surprised as I was, though neither of us showed it. A glance passed between us before I turned away. Johnny had all the help he needed, and seeing there was a badge pinned to his shirt, I wasn't sure that he wanted to claim me as any kind of friend. Like Johnny, I had done a few lawless things in my time, but my efforts were more recent. As I went away from there I heard him yelling questions about his horse. I could have told him that the Arabian was still spooked but otherwise all right. What I didn't have to tell him was that he wouldn't be walking for quite some time.

Nothing is deader than a small town on a Sunday afternoon. This one was deader than most. Dragoon Wells had seen better days but not lately. It must have bustled pretty good when the mines were working; now it was just a town drowsing in the sun.

There were two hotels and one was boarded up, sun and wind taking their toll. The other hotel, right across the street, was open for business, but there was no mob of room seekers breaking down the door to get in. The door was open and I raised a man from the dead, namely the clerk from his Sunday afternoon nap, and got a key to a room for two dollars.

The clerk was interested in me, but not enough to start throwing questions. He turned the register on its swivel and gawked at my name before he settled back in his chair and spread a bandanna over his face. A potted palm and a lot of flies had died in the lobby; that's about all there was, and maybe the rest of the paying guests were at the races.

The room was No. 5 and there was a brass bed, the usual boxwood furniture. The flowered wallpaper was stained and faded. I had been in too many hotel rooms like this one; it didn't bother me. I put my stuff on the dresser and stretched out on the bed.

I hadn't been there much more than an hour when somebody rapped on the door. I knew it wasn't Callahan. A kid with arms and legs all loose like a rag doll came in.

"Marshall Callahan wants to talk to you," he said, shifting from one foot to the other. That didn't suit him; so he shifted back. "Quick as you can he'd like to."

"You sure you got the right room and the right man?" I wanted to know what name Johnny was calling me by. In the West a lot of wanted men go by the name of John Ryan. Not Smith—Ryan—and don't ask me why.

"You're Jim Saddler, ain't you?" the kid said.

I nodded. "Where do I find him?"

The kid said the jail. "He'd be obliged you came right

8

now," he said. "The marshal don't like to be kept waiting."

I found the jail without the kid's help. It had been built when the town was a town, intended to remain a town; a brick building of fair size, barred windows, iron banded oak door with old reward posters tacked up on both sides of it, a porch and a rocker.

A doctor was finishing up with Johnny when I went in. He was all splinted up and riding an old wheelchair with cobwebs still on it. A bottle and a glass stood on the desk with the usual lawman's office junk.

It was a good-looking jail; good looking as Johnny himself. The damn place was painted and swept out; the wide planked floor had been ground smooth and oiled until it glistened. It smelled of good cigars and good whiskey, none of that puke-and-sweat smell you get in jails. The desk wasn't the usual boot-scarred article but a heavy polished oak job with brass knobs for the drawers. The whole place gave me the feeling that old Johnny was doing all right for himself.

We just nodded. No hand pumping or back slapping. "Take a chair, be with you when the doc gets through."

I sat and listened and the doctor, an irritable old man, was laying down the law. "By rights you ought to be in bed," he said. "Why the hell do you want to sit a chair when you can be in your bed?"

Johnny said, "Cause I don't like bed except for two things. Right now I don't feel like neither. Now tell me the rest of it. Maybe I'll even believe you."

"Makes no difference what you do," the doctor snapped. "You got two broken legs. Nice clean breaks. You're young enough so all you have to do is let the bones knit. That's what you're supposed to do. Bang those legs around and you'll be walking on sticks the rest of your life."

"What's wrong with the wheelchair?" Johnny said.

"Not a thing when you're ready for it. My guess is you'll be glad to get to bed after a while. I'm leaving some

9

laudanum if the pain gets bad. It's not whiskey, Marshal, you take it by the spoonful. Don't take too much, just what I said, or you won't have to worry about the legs or anything else. You'll be dead. Send the boy if you need me."

"Ain't this a bitch!" Johnny said after the doctor packed his bag and left. Johnny drummed on the splints with his fingertips. "What in hell are you doing here, Saddler?"

"The kid said you wanted to see me, didn't like to be kept waiting." I grinned at Johnny, his fancy duds still dusty from the fall, at the worried look on his lean, handsome face. Johnny must have some Indian blood in him. He's dark and has crow black hair with a shine to it. His light blue eyes were the Callahan part.

"I mean what are you doing in Dragoon Wells?" Johnny said. "You wouldn't be dodging the law, by any chance? For something big enough for them to start looking for you here? No need to get your back up about it, just asking."

"Nobody's looking for me that I know of," I said. "A few places I wouldn't be welcome, no more than that. Since you're asking, how about you? You haven't been heard from these last few years."

Johnny laughed and grimaced with pain at the same time. "Hell no!" he said. "It happened I found a good thing here and decided to stick with it. I'm a pillar of the community, more or less. There's some here wouldn't cry if I moved on, but never get up the nerve to say it. Others don't mind me; I do a good job for the town."

I looked around the well-kept office, at Johnny himself. "You look like you do a few things for yourself."

Johnny's smile was modest and that was worse than bragging. "A few creature comforts, Jim, old pardner."

My fur went up when I heard that old pardner stuff. Johnny is the kind who can be charming without being friendly, a good kind to watch out for. I was watching out real hard.

10

"You have something in mind, or did you want to talk about the horse race?" I enquired.

"What's your hurry? You sound like you're not glad to see me."

"Sure I am, Johnny," I said. "How the hell are you?"

"Got two broken legs," Johnny answered. "Otherwise good. How's about you?"

I told Johnny a few of the things I'd been doing. The big poker game I came out a big winner from in Sandstream, New Mexico. The rich girl I busted loose from a gang of outlaws in the Colorado mountains.

For a moment, Johnny looked homesick for the rootless life he used to lead. Then it passed as I knew it would. Johnny had that comfortable look that comes early to some men, even if they aren't married. When it isn't marriage it's money, and I had a fair idea that Johnny wasn't married.

"I don't know," Johnny said. "All this moving about, it's not all that great."

I didn't agree with that. I like to move around. "Looks like you're through with it," I said. "Me, I'm on my way to Sonora. I'll see when I get there."

Johnny wheeled himself around to the other side of the desk and pushed the chair out of the way. Then he got another glass from the drawer and filled that one and the one on the desk. It was Jack Daniel's, good stuff, no need of water. I got mine and knocked it back and got another one.

"That's what I wanted to talk to you about," Johnny said, getting out a box of long nines for both of us. We lit up and Johnny said, "Don't sound like you got pressing business in Mexico."

I can dicker too. "I'd like to get there," I said.

"Where the money is."

Johnny nodded and did the honors again. "That's the place to be. Of course there's money all over if you know how to get at it."

"And you do?"

11

"I'm getting good at it," Johnny said. "There's money here; you can have some if you like."

I said I'd like to get in the way of making some money. "What do I have to do to get it?"

"Work for me is what. I'm going to be needing a deputy. You could be him."

I had another drink to see if I liked the idea. I didn't. "I'd feel foolish," I said. "Look foolish, feel foolish. Thanks for thinking of me, but the answer has to be no. Look, old pardner, if you were in a real fix I'd probably help you out for old time's sake. You and me and the folks back home. But you're not. Tell me what's so hard about finding another deputy?"

"What's so hard? Hard as hell to find the right man. I need a man I can trust."

"What makes you sure you can trust me?"

Johnny smiled. "About this I think I can."

"You mean I wouldn't be after your job?"

"Exactly right. You'll never settle down and you know it. If you were a sensible man you'd find something the way I did. I do just fine in this village. The marshal's pay isn't too much, but I got a few sidelines. Got a handle on the poker games in town, faro as well. The man that runs a few girls upstairs over the saloon is kind of a partner. You could say I got a few investments here and there."

"What did you invest?"

"My goodwill," Johnny said, smiling. "No, sir, it's not what you're thinking. I didn't stomp in there and tell folks here's your new equal-share partner. Plenty of lawmen do that, but that makes for bad feeling all round. You do that to a man and he's going to have the knife ready for you if you stumble."

"You did more than stumble today. Where's the knife?"

Johnny waved away the smoke from his cigar. "So far it's only a small knife. Let me lay it out for you fair and honest. In some towns they got lawmen so mean, so crooked, the only way they can get rid of them is to kill them. Hire some gunslinger just as bad to do the job. Hire him and hope he won't decide to take over where the dead man left off. You know me, Jim. I like money because I never had none. The thing is, I know how far I can go. I cleaned up their town for them and haven't robbed them blind. I faced the killers and did away with the ones that wouldn't run. No help in the doing of it, just me."

"But they still don't like you?"

"That's too strong," Johnny said. "I doubt they'd hire a gun to kill me. When I was taming the town I drew top wages. But I didn't hold them up for the same wages when the town got quiet. I got them together and said I was going to work for half of what I'd been getting."

I had to smile at Johnny's gall. "What had you been getting? Four hundred a month?"

Johnny smiled too. "Five," he said. "I'm a good man. Still, I did cut back by half. All right, I didn't lose anything after I started getting my contributions from the games and the girls, other things. Even got me a sweet little horse ranch outside town. You saw that Arabian I was riding today. That's just one of my fine animals."

"How much do I get?" I asked. I knew Johnny would try to beat me on the money, but I didn't want him to get too Scotch about it.

"A minute ago you didn't want the job."

"You talked me into it," I said. "How much is my share?"

Johnny looked at me with the suspicion of a wealthy widow, a rich fat lady of 60 faced with a man half her age who had just sworn his undying love. "Your share, as you call it, ain't half. If that's what you're thinking, then my answer is no. What did you have in mind, Jim, old pardner?"

There he went again. I did some adding and subtracting in my head, estimated how much Johnny squeezed from the pimps and the gamblers, then added about a quarter more than I expected to get. I gave out the figure, adding, "If you need me as bad as you say—" I didn't say the rest.

Johnny got ready to bluff it, then changed his mind. "The fact is, I do need you to back me. Not just back me, hold down the job for me. The doc was right about the pain. I don't know how long I'm going to be able to ride this thing. I'm going to have to work into it like the doc says. So it's bed for me, for a while. The minute that happens they're going to appoint a deputy of their own. I know how these fat merchants work. They'll hire some local shithead for less than half what I'm getting. Somebody tough but dumb they think they can handle. They could even promise him the job permanent if he can run me out of town. With me in this thing"—Johnny beat on the arms of the wheelchair—"that wouldn't take much doing."

"It could be done," I agreed. "What's your offer, boss?"

We beat on the money until it took a shape we both liked. I was to get half Johnny's wages, plus 20 per-cent of his take from the girls and the gambling, ten per-cent from the whiskey business. That was slow at times, Johnny swore up and down, and I didn't believe him but I took it. Nothing would be due to me from the horse ranch because it wasn't making any money.

Johnny set up drinks to clinch the deal. "A month here will set you up just fine," he said, losing his worried look. "And the nice thing about it, you don't have to do a damn thing. About the only excitement we see here is when some cowhand or farmer gets drunk. Then you lock him up, more than one if you're lucky, and collect a fine for drunk and disorderly the next morning. Collect the fine as soon as they open their eyes. Water's free but I don't serve breakfast. No, sir, and you can stop looking at me like that. It's none of your business what I collect from the town to feed prisoners. You get your wages and that's it."

I smiled at this guardian of law and order. "I didn't say

a thing," I said.

"You didn't have to. What the hell, the fines are just small potatoes. You'll get a fair shake from me and I know you'll give me the same."

"If the money adds up right."

"That's what I meant," Johnny said. "This is the tastiest little gravy boat you ever dipped into, old pardner. Make it look good for me and I'll never forget you. Don't get too rough with the people. They're good folks, most of them. Make your rounds on time, rattle the door locks on the stores, give them the feeling of being secure. That's what I do. You're going to get fat on this job, old pardner. You got anything else you want to thrash out?"

"One small thing," I said.

Johnny looked suspicious again. "What would that be, old pardner?"

"What you just said. That old pardner business. Do me a favor and drop it."

It wasn't costing money so Johnny smiled. "Sure thing, Deputy Saddler. Which reminds me, you got to swear and so forth. Then you get a badge."

I swore to uphold the laws of this and that. "You're supposed to keep a straight face," Johnny complained as he pinned on my deputy marshal's badge.

"That's asking too much," I said.

TWO

Kate Flannery came to town during my second day on the job. After that the job was never the same.

The first day was dead as dust. The only excitement was the look on the town fathers' faces when Johnny announced that I was going to be the new deputy. He asked for a meeting of the town council, so called, so he could give them the good news, and I have to say this for them—they didn't jump for joy. Far from it. There was a lot of throat clearing and sidelong glances before a burly banker named Dougal McLandress, a man with an air of importance as big as his belly, ventured the opinion that Marshal Callahan might have asked their advice before he pinned the deputy badge on me.

"What do we know about this man?" McLandress said, and those with nerve enough backed him up. Some of the town fathers didn't seem too concerned about me, and I figured they were the ones who didn't have to part with any money to keep Johnny in race horses. Even so, there was considerable opposition to the idea of making me assistant lawdog of Dragoon Wells.

Johnny, the old West Texas fox, didn't get tough about it. I knew he would if he had to; at the moment, he didn't. "I'll stake my reputation on Jim Saddler," he said. "A finer man never lived than my friend here. Jim was a big help to me in the taming of many wild towns."

"Where was that?" McLandress wanted to know.

"All over," Johnny said before he went on to tell more lies about me. "You can sleep safe in your beds with Jim Saddler watching over the town. Jim Saddler will die on his feet before he lets any harm come to you."

"What can happen here?" McLandress argued. "Why not appoint a local man? Plenty men here could use the work." That was an appeal to local sentiment and the banker got some response. Some of the town fathers muttered for a while.

Johnny waited until they got through, then he said, "You raise two good points, Mr. McLandress. What can happen here, you want to know. The answer is, you never know. As soon as word gets out that I'm laid up, it could be that certain parties could take a notion to head this way. You ever notice they don't rob banks in busy towns, Mr. McLandress. The quiet towns they go after. It could happen. Then where would your local deputy be? Most likely he'd be dead and your bank would be empty."

McLandress grunted at the wound in his wallet. "The point is, you should have told us."

"I'm telling you now," Johnny repeated. "A local man wouldn't have the know-how, is what I mean. I'm not saying Jim Saddler is the only good man in the Territory. I'm saying he's good and he's here. Jim's my new deputy, gentlemen. I wouldn't trade him no matter what."

At last, the gloves were off and Johnny was showing how hard his fist was.

McLandress hooked his thumbs in his brocaded vest and rocked back on his heels, the very picture of a man of substance. It was plain that he was the most important man in that one-horse town; not getting his way didn't suit him.

"Then you won't reconsider?" he asked pompously, making the floorboards creak with his weight.

Johnny's light blue eyes hardened just enough to back up what he told the banker and everyone there. "Nothing to consider. Deputy Saddler's already sworn in. You're going to like him fine, you'll see."

Johnny didn't laugh until they got outside. "That's how you have to handle the sons of bitches. McLandress there would like to punch a hole in my kettle, doesn't know how to do it. Which doesn't mean he won't keep trying. You're here to see he doesn't. Now you can do what you like, I'm for bed. How in hell am I going to do a woman with these things on my legs?"

"Use your head, Johnny," I suggested.

"Like the New Orleans Frenchmen do?" Johnny sounded dubious about the idea. That would be his West Texas Baptist upbringing.

"Nothing wrong with it," I said, thinking of a few sweet little fillies who liked it that way. "You don't have to be French to like it. Make a trade. You do it to her, let her do it to you."

Texas may be a big state but old Johnny, the Panhandle shitkicker, hadn't been around that much. "You ever try it that way?"

"Anything worth doing is worth trying," I said. "First time I tried it convinced me."

Just then the loose-limbed kid came into the jail and said the buggy was waiting outside.

Johnny looked surprised. "What in hell are you talking about, Calvin?"

"Doc Kline said you'd be needing it along about now," Calvin said. "You don't want it?"

Johnny turned to me grinning through his pain. "That old quack knows too much. Anything comes up, send this fool out to fetch me."

18

"That's me he's talking about," Calvin said, holding the door open so Johnny could wheel himself through.

"You're on your own, Jim," Johnny said and went out.

I felt like a fool, honest I did. There I was with a star on my chest and a town to protect. I have nothing much against lawmen, nothing for them neither. Mostly, when I can do it, I keep the hell away from them, and it makes no difference to me if they're straight or crooked. I like them best when they're like Johnny, a little of both. If the story ever got out, me being a lawman, I would have to take a lot of joshing from the hard people I know. But, hell, I could always deny it; right then I was just interested in the money.

After I got my first look at Kate Flannery, money took a back seat. I opened the jail door and there she was, a vision with red hair in a green dress, going past in a new-looking black buggy with red and gold paint work. It glittered in spite of the trail dust, and so did she. Perched on top of her head was a dark silk hat the same color as her dress. If a swan could take human form, she'd be it; she had the same lift and curve of the neck and was proud as bejesus.

It was getting on toward sundown and the sun was a glow instead of a glare. She knew she was making an entrance, as the people say, and you never saw a nicer one.

A glossy black horse was pulling the buggy, and proud to do it. The gold glow of the sun hit her eyes when she looked at me. I had a feeling they'd be green, but that wasn't all of it. Anybody can have green eyes, but these were the real green eyes of a real redhead. You see eyes like that three or four times in a lifetime and you never forget them.

Women always know their good points and, while Kate had many, her eyes were the best. They flickered over me, deciding what I was in a glance; cool, scornful, they saw all they wanted to see. The people came out to gawk at her and with every good reason: Kate was

19

something to stare at, a woman to arouse hatred and envy in women, a woman for loveless, horny men to dream about.

I was proud of myself because I was the only one there who got a glance, an indication that I existed. Most likely that was because she hadn't seen me before. The others she ignored, as she sat in the spring seat, handling the well-trained horse with a queenly air. It was quiet, with the light about to go, but I could feel the excitement. She wasn't a stranger to these people, these dead-brained town dwellers. They knew her and didn't like her and some there hated her. I thought she was wonderful; that's how I am. I'm what they call a romantic, meaning that I'd rather look at a beautiful woman than eat dinner. This one was wild for all her ladylike airs. Her wildness came out and grabbed you, shocked you like a burn—a nice shock. I liked it at the time, and for all that happened later, I went on liking it. I liked it so much it nearly got me killed.

Then she passed from sight and Dragoon Wells was dull and dead again. Dust kicked up by the carriage swirled in the sun shafts of early evening. For a while there was nothing but the smooth noise of the passing carriage; after that was gone conversation buzzed up loud like disturbed bees. Whoever this green-eyed woman was, she was of some interest in my town.

My town! I liked the sound of that, if only in my head. There was no special reason to carry a rifle on my rounds, but I did it anyway, just to let them know. Now they had me to gawk at, though I wasn't half as pretty. They were still crowding the sidewalks, still buzzing when I went by. A few nodded stiffly, others just looked.

Dragoon Wells had been Mexican before it was American, and some of the old influence lingered in the wide plaza, the old Spanish church, the few dark faces left. The barbershop was called the City Barber Shop, Amos Parkins, *Prop.* A few streets straggled off the main drag, small houses painted white, some not. Everything was closed up except the three saloons, but business wasn't booming. A few horses were hitched in front. Along the main street a few shade trees were left. The ones I saw looked sorry to be there.

I made a tour of the town with everybody watching me. I don't know what they expected to see, but that's how they are in small towns. They say it takes man biting dog to make news in the big city; in a place like Dragoon Wells, dog biting dog is pretty hot stuff. Banker McLandress was out parading with his wife and daughter. I guessed she was his daughter, though there was no resemblance to mother or father. A good thing for her too. How these two lardy, suet-faced people ever produced a raving beauty like Laurie McLandress was one of the great mysteries of the world.

Of course she wasn't introduced to me by her first name. In fact, she wouldn't have been introduced at all if I hadn't pushed it. I think it would have pleased the fat banker if there had been a doorway or a side street to turn into, but there wasn't, and when I tipped my hat he felt he had to go through with it.

McLandress had a fat man's way of puffing out his words, as if he could never get enough breath. That gave him an abrupt manner of speaking that was just right for his natural bad temperedness.

"This is my wife and daughter, Mr. Saddler," he said. "Out for our before-Sunday-supper walk, as you can see."

I could see the daughter, all I wanted to see. Dragoon Wells wasn't such a dead town after all—two beautiful women inside of ten minutes. Not that Kate Flannery and Laurie McLandress had much in common, on the outside. Well no, I take that back. They looked different, but they had a lot in common. All beautiful women do, and I don't mean their looks, though everything else spins off from there. Laurie was dark haired and black eyed. Her eyes were not Spanish eyes, not black soulful eyes, but bright and clear, maybe a little hard. Her face was heart shaped and there was a sly, some would say mean, turn to her mouth. Her voice surprised me. It was Southern whereas her parents sounded like Yankees. It wasn't until later that I learned she had just come back from a finishing school in Charleston.

"And how do you like our fair city, Mr. Saddler?" she asked. Like her mouth, everything she said had a mean, humorous twist to it, and in a woman less beautiful, it would have been hard to take. But I'm a fool for beautiful women, and they can do just about anything to me except kill me.

"I like it fine, Miss McLandress," I said, wondering what she would be like in bed, then deciding that she need not be anything but there. I wanted to find out about the redhead in the buggy, but Laurie or her parents were not the people to ask.

She gave me the information anyway. "The town isn't usually this lively on Sunday evening," she said, smiling. "Did you get to see the reason?"

"Laurie!" old McLandress chided. "It's got nothing to do with us. Besides—"

"Oh fudge!" Laurie said, making "fudge" sound like something else. "The deputy is a man, isn't he? Did you see her, Deputy?"

"Would that be a lady in a shiny black buggy?"

"Well yes," he said, turning on her wicked smile again. "The *woman* in the buggy. How did you like her?"

In proportion, Mrs. McLandress was just as bulky as her husband, and a real stuffed shirtwaist. "Really, Laurie," she said. "I'm sure what the Flannery girl does is none of the deputy's concern. Isn't that right, Mr. Saddler?"

"Just as long as she doesn't break any laws," I said sternly.

Mrs. McLandress scolded Laurie for laughing in public. "There's nothing to laugh about," she said.

Laurie's bell-like laugh dwindled down to a smile. "You're wrong, Mama. I think what the deputy said is very funny, and I think the deputy knows it's funny. Don't you, Deputy?"

"Nothing is funny where the law is concerned, Miss McLandress," I said as sanctimoniously as before.

That earned me a curt nod of approval from the banker, more giggling from the daughter. "Marshal Callahan is funny and doesn't know it. Mr. Saddler is funny and won't admit it," Laurie said. "I like you better than Marshal Callahan, Mr. Saddler."

All this was said in that apple pan dowdy voice that seems made for pretty women with brains who don't want to let on how smart they are. This one was bright and catty, but with her looks and that husky voice I forgave her everything, even for a few things that hadn't happened yet. I had a feeling they would.

Laurie was whisked away to Sunday supper before she had a chance to say anything else. I guessed she was all of 19, a full-grown woman where I was raised. Out in my part of the country they are having their third kid at that age. The man who got Laurie McLandress was in for soft nights and hard days, for she had the look of a woman who would drive a man hard, in or out of bed. She might kill him young but he'd know he'd been alive. I wondered what she was doing in Dragoon Wells. From where I stood she looked like a rose on a dunghill, as out of place as she could get. I hoped she wasn't just home for a visit. Of course there was always the redhead to think about. Like they say, variety is the spice—and I was feeling spicy as a stallion.

I finished my rounds without seeing any more pretty women. Sure I saw women, but if you put pants on them they could have been men. The West is hard on women, and I'm not faulting them for having lantern jaws and skin like cured cowhide. I know that many a good heart beats behind a bony chest; usually I don't get to look that far.

Johnny had asked me to look in on the poker games at the Dorado Saloon, and that's what I did. Two middling-stakes games were going, not bad for a Sunday night in the middle of nowhere. As soon as I pushed open the door a small, city-looking man wearing a candy-striped shirt with rosette armbands reached across the bar and insisted on pumping my hand. I guessed he was the owner and he said he was.

"Floyd Casey's my name," he said while he still had my hand. "A shame what happened to Johnny the Gent, ain't it." He didn't sound too broken up about it.

"Terrible," I said.

Casey threw me a quick, foxy look which turned out to be the only look he had. "A few things maybe we can talk about. I mean later when you get settled," he began cautiously.

"I know what you mean," I said, giving nothing away. I knew what he meant. Johnny's partner in the girl and whiskey and gambling business was feeling me out for a double cross. Right then, that was as far as it got.

Casey reached under the bar and brought out his private bottle and set out drinks. That bourbon was so smooth it would have cured a sore throat. We had another one and Casey said, "You see a good-looking redhead in a buggy just now?"

"Kate Flannery?" I said.

"Not Carrie Nation," Casey said. "You get a good look at her? Sure you did. Ain't she something now. Wait till Johnny the Gent hears she's back in town. Of course I forget you ain't from these parts and don't know a thing about it. I'm giving away no secrets when I say that Johnny used to be stuck real hard on Kate. Something went on between them, I don't know what. Before she had a big row with her father and run off, there was bad feeling between her and Johnny. Least they didn't talk but there was a time when they was thick as sour milk. Never did get to know who did the breaking off, her or Johnny. It'd be worth a man's life to ask him. Johnny's good natured enough, not about that gal though. I wonder what in hell she's doing back here. Always said, not to me, she'd wash dirty shirts before she ever came back to Dragoon Wells."

"How long has she been away?" I asked, thinking I might as well get Casey's version of it. There were bound to be others. I got the feeling that this Kate Flannery, so beautiful and by all reports so ornery, was going to be trouble. Don't ask me how I knew because I didn't. It was just a feeling, but I've learned to trust my hunches in some things. Besides, I know women pretty good. I've known my share of them.

"The best part of two years," Casey said. "She was gone before anybody knew it. It came out though. One of the Flannery boys got drunk in town, unusual enough, they never come to town more than they have to. Later the talk was she'd hooked up with Peyton Ballard down in Mexico."

Now there was a name to wake up a conversation. "You mean the outlaw?" I asked, knowing there couldn't be two Peyton Ballards. Twenty years before, Peyton Ballard had been the most wanted Confederate guerrilla in the Southwest. All through the war he plundered and killed, waving the Stars and Bars all the time he was doing it. When Grant said the Confederates could take their side arms and go home he didn't include Peyton Ballard. Ulysses S. made it a personal order: catch Peyton Ballard and hang him on the spot.

"Some folks don't see him as an outlaw," Casey said, pouring whiskey. "The Secesh crowd think of him as a hard man in a hard time. But not a bandit. There's some that tried to get him a pardon so he can come back from Sonora."

Sonora was only a few days' ride from where we were. I said, "That where he is, the bloody-handed bastard?"

Casey pushed the bottle to me. "That's where he is, best I know. Makes no difference to me where he is, what he done. I'm in the saloon business, I keep out of wars. They tell me he stayed on in the Territory for a few years after the war. Rallied a bunch of die-hard Rebs, swore

25

they'd never surrender. They swore they'd fight the bluebellies but most of the fighting was done in banks and stage robberies. Finally the army made it so hot for him he dodged on south and stayed there. Was rich when he left, is richer now."

"You think there's something to the story about the Flannery girl?"

"Could be," Casey said. "Here's how the story was told to me. Kate was traveling with some well-heeled Mexican who died or got killed someplace in Sonora. So she was stranded in some town and that's where Ballard found her. Maybe it was in Durango. That name comes to me. It's a big cowtown, so it figures Ballard would be there. He's a big rancher now, what I hear. More than a rancher, has horse herds and sells mounts to the Mex army. Mines, land, and such. Is a close friend of important politicians, both sides of the border. They say he'd still like to come back."

Casey stopped talking and looked at me, blowing a silent whistle as he did. "You're thinking the same thing, ain't you?"

"Maybe," I said, looking down at the badge on my chest. All of a sudden it wasn't a joke anymore. "Ballard has the name of holding on to what he thinks belongs to him. No need to get worked up about it, I guess. Likely enough it's just another wild story."

But the foxy little saloonkeeper wasn't fooled by my offhand manner. Grinning hard, he said, "That's what it is, just a story. Nothing is ever going to happen in this town."

He didn't believe it, and neither did I.

THREE

The smell of a woman's body can get me hard before you can count to ten. I opened the door of the jail and there it was in the darkness, faint but unmistakable, and it hadn't been there when I went out. It came fresh and clean through the cigar and bourbon smells. But I brought my gun out because a woman can kill as quickly as a man. I stepped in and away from the door, then Laurie McLandress said in that husky Southern voice, "Why don't you lock the door before you light the lamp. I already shut the shutters."

I touched the wick with a match and yellow light flared up. Laurie was behind the desk looking beautiful with a whiskey glass in her hand. I put the rifle in the rack.

Laurie said, "I haven't broken any laws and I haven't come to confess. Aren't you going to ask me why I did come?" She slid the bottle across the desk.

"You'll tell me when you get around to it," I said. Suddenly, I was as relaxed as she was. This was just a little sparring to be gone through. You ever see the way pigeons mate? I guess everybody has. The female minces about with bitty steps while the male puffs out his chest and circles her, still pecking away but getting closer all the time. Pigeons know what they're doing, and so did we. However, this was a young lady of refinement, so I didn't just unbutton my pants. But that's where she was looking, unbuttoned or not. I didn't want to stand there bulging, so I sat down on the customer's side of my own desk.

"My father would kill me if he found me here," she informed me, not sounding too worried about it. It was hard to think of fat-assed McLandress killing anybody, but I knew he'd talk a lot. McLandress was the kind that couldn't say good morning without sounding indignant about it.

"Then we won't tell him," I said.

"Tell me about yourself," Laurie said casually, going at the whiskey again, drinking like a veteran. "If you don't mind, that is. I like to know something about a man before I get . . . confidential . . . with him. I have an idea what you're like. Why don't you tell me more?"

I told her what I was. That didn't mean that she wouldn't come back and say that I'd deceived her. Women do what they feel like doing. You have to be ready for it, as ready as you can. You're never ready enough.

I didn't make a book out of the telling and she liked that. Naturally I didn't tell her everything, just the good parts. "See, I was right," she said. "You're a wild, reckless man. You could be mean to a woman, but she'd have to provoke you. How would you like to be provoked?"

I stood up and she came around the desk to meet me. "I'd like it," I said. As I reached for her, she said, "We'll talk later, all right."

Anything she did was jake with me. I just didn't want her to leave. I didn't ask myself why she was there. It was enough that she was, soft and willing, and what else she was could wait till later. What she did next hadn't been learned in that Charleston finishing school. Her hand went down to my crotch and she said, "Ah yes!" when she touched it. Then she unbuttoned me while my hands squeezed her rounded young ass. She took my cock out and rubbed it gently while I unbuttoned the back of her dress. It fell to the floor and she kicked it to one side. She had come prepared: she was naked under the dress. I stood there with my cock between her legs, running my hands over her, and she said, "It would be ever so much nicer lying down, don't you think?"

I picked her up and kneed open the door to the back room and carried her in. It was a small room with a bed, and I wondered if Kate Flannery had been there with Johnny. I put her down on the soft quilt, and she pulled me down after her. Now, she couldn't get me into her fast enough; and she pulled my hands away and took charge of my cock, guiding it in straight and true. She was wet and I went in all the way, and her spine arched with pleasure. I knew she wanted more than this; at the moment it was enough. She came almost immediately and that was just the salad.

Light from the office seeped into the room, and I could see the sweet, sweaty shine of her soft young body. Her polished black hair came loose and tumbled about her shoulders, and her face was very young. But there was nothing maidenly about what she did to me, or maybe there was. It wasn't her first time and I was glad about that. Virgins don't excite me the way they do other men. She came three times before she whispered, "Please let me feel you coming. Fill me up with your hot, sweet juice." She gave little yelps of delight when I drove into her and shot my load; she would have clapped her hands if they hadn't been digging into my thighs.

We lay there, my weight on top of her slender body. She begged me not to take my cock out of her, but to leave it in her warm wetness where it would get hard again in a little while. I was only too glad to leave it where it was. Now and then she would contract her muscles down there and give it a squeeze that sent shivers up and down my spine. I groaned a little every time she did it and that pleased her because she knew how much pleasure she was giving. But she wasn't like some young girls who keep asking, "Is it good? Is it good? Am I doing it right?" She didn't have to ask anything because she knew it was good and she was doing it exactly right. I wasn't ready to go yet, but it was nice to lie like that.

Now it was her turn to moan as I sucked her soft yet firm breasts, sweet as cherries. "Oh Jesus!" she called out. "You're driving me crazy—but don't stop. Make me come, Saddler. Make me flow. I want it to pour out of me. I want you to think your cock is sliding in a bath of warm honey." She giggled at the thought. She was as horny as all get-out, but she was also young and full of mischief.

I was hard enough to start pumping again, so I pumped and sucked at the same time, while my hands kneaded her girlish ass. She locked her slender legs around the small of my back and ground her crotch into mine. I fucked her steadily, not brutally but steadily, drawing my shaft almost all the way out, then driving it to the hilt. The juice poured out of her until her pussy was sopping wet. A good sex smell was everywhere in the room, exciting both of us almost as much as the fucking itself, and it did feel like I was driving my shaft into a tight little tunnel lubricated with warm honey.

It was the best kind of what they call a honey-fuck—the kind where you're fucking somebody you really like and not some faceless whore you'll never see again. It was so damn good with her and could only get better. She hadn't sucked my cock yet, and I hadn't tongued her, but it was early and there was plenty of time for that. I kept on pumping, wanting to get the most out of it, wanting her to have the same intense pleasure. She took my face in both hands and held it, staring and smiling at the same time, as if she really wanted to see who was doing this to her.

She kissed me and put her tongue in my mouth. Doing that topped everything off, and she came and came and came, mumbling with her tongue still in my mouth. She had been wet before, but now the warm juice flowed out of her hot cunt and down her thighs. Now it was slippery between her legs and it couldn't have been better. There's nothing wrong with lust, and my cock got bigger, the wetter she got. Again she whispered that she wanted me to come and I needed no encouragement. I came until it seemed I could come no more. I felt drained and relaxed. This time I pulled out of her and we lay side by side. She closed her eyes and squeezed her legs together and sighed.

"I do that in bed at night," she said softly. "You won't think I'm bad if I tell you sometimes I get so excited I have to use my finger to make myself come?"

"Why should I think that makes you bad?"

"I just thought it might. My mother does and has warned me against it. I know she looks at my sheets for evidence of wetness. But I fooled her. Since she got suspicious, I've been putting a towel under me so I won't stain the sheets when I come. You know how wet I get."

"I do."

"You don't mind that?"

"Course not. It shows you've been having a good time."

"I like the way you say that: been having a good time. It sounds so nice and natural, as if there's nothing sinful about it."

"Sinful? That's foolish talk," I told her.

Laurie said, "You don't know my parents. Everything is sinful to them. Most dances are sinful. Most books are sinful. I once asked Daddy—he eats an awful lot—what about gluttony and he got mad. They've got sin on the brain."

"They must have done something to get you."

31

Holding onto my shaft, Laurie giggled. "I'll bet Daddy felt it was his duty. Do it, get it over with, but don't enjoy it. I'll bet they fucked with their nightgowns on. That's the kind they are. I love them, but they don't enjoy life. If they could only see me now."

"I'd just as soon they didn't." I was glad the iron-banded jail door was locked and barred. There would be no way to deal with old McLandress if he managed to break in.

"Don't worry about that," Laurie said. "They think I'm all tucked in for the night. Safe in my chaste little bed. Mother always warns me to say my prayers before I go to sleep. Well, you know what I think of that. Prick not prayer is what I think of before I close my eyes. The first time I saw you I knew you had a big one. I dreamt about you when I took my nap. Do you ever dream about pussy?"

"Sometimes I do," I said honestly. "It makes for sweeter dreams."

Laurie turned to look at me. "Do you ever come when you're having one of those dreams?"

Jesus! Such a conversation! "Not since I was a kid. Most kids have wet dreams. You stop having them when you get older and real life women are available."

Laurie giggled again. "I'm available," she said, and stretched out and took my cock in her mouth. She had a small tender mouth and my throbbing cock filled it completely. I don't know where a young girl like that learned to suck cocks so expertly. Maybe it came naturally to her. She sucked and used her tongue at the same time. I came and she swallowed it.

There was no awkwardness after it was over, as happens when strangers get to it without much love talk. Laurie sat up in the bed, groping in it for hairpins, while I fetched drinks.

"It was just fine," she said with hairpins in her mouth. I waited with the drink until she finished pinning back her hair. She smelled of clean sweat and soap and toilet water, and when I kissed her she smelled of bourbon. She told me that she had been born in Vermont, that the family came to Arizona because of her brother Tad's bad chest. Arizona hadn't helped Tad, and he had died. Old McLandress had been a banker in Vermont, and he followed the same trade in the Southwest. He was richer than people thought he was, Laurie said. Even if he lost half his money he'd still be rolling in green.

"I love my Papa and everything, but he's too strict," Laurie said. "That's why he sent me to that school in Charleston. Would you believe it, we're Scotch Presbyterians and he sent me to a school run by *nuns!* Next thing to a convent. I had to go to school with a lot of rich *Catholics!*"

"That's terrible," I agreed.

Laurie stroked me as if we'd been doing this for a long time. "Don't make fun," she said. "It was awful. The only fun I had was when I went over the wall after lights out. There was another girl and we'd go in the city— there are places, you know. Would you believe, a very, very handsome French teacher lost his position because of me. His apparatus was rather small. So he was not all that exciting. But you are. You are very exciting, yes you are. What's the use of living if you can't have fun. You think I'm terrible, don't you?"

I said not a bit of it.

"Well, I am glad to hear that," Laurie went on. "My father doesn't believe in a person having fun. We're not put on this earth to have fun, he says. My God! Now he's mad because I don't want to get married. You should see some of the men that come around, or he brings around. Oh I grant you some of them are pretty rich and one isn't bad looking. But you know, I'll be rich too when my father dies, but I just know the stuffy old dear will live practically forever. I keep saying to myself, if only you had your inheritance *now!*"

Sweet Jesus Christ! I was in bed with a girl who wanted to murder her old man! I asked her about it. She laughed so hard the bed shook, and she pushed and tugged at me until I nearly fell on the floor. "You're crazy!" she laughed. "I wouldn't do *that!* You must think . . . oh, I don't believe it. No, no, I'm just talking about money."

"Sure you are," I said.

"The thing is, if I had my inheritance instead of having to wait for it, everything would be wonderful. Those men, I wouldn't even have to think about marrying one of them. It wouldn't even be dishonest, the money is mine anyway. It's in my father's will, the old darling. I saw it, he showed it to me. His entire estate is to be divided equally between my mother and me. Of course I'm going to need help."

"To do what?"

"Take the money out of the bank and get away with it. My father has more cash than he needs to cover it. So no one has to know. I'll just leave a note explaining everything. And I won't be greedy. I don't want more than I'm legally entitled to. My share will take care of your share. I have keys to everything."

My glass was empty so I drank from hers. "If it's that easy, why do you need me?"

"Silly! Of course I need you. You think I'd feel safe going away with all that money? A woman alone in this god-awful country. I'd be nervous, but you're not nervous. We could go away together I don't know where. You pick a place. What about Mexico City or Havana? The nice thing, we'd have the money and we'd have us."

"You forget I'm a lawman," I said, and we both laughed and hung all over each other. Sex may be the best fun you can have without laughing, but we were laughing too. She was crazy as a coot and she was close to being rich. Rich and one of the finest women that ever rumpled a bed.

"I'll have to think about it," I said.

"Oh shit!" Laurie said. "If you're worrying about Callahan, he'll be all right. He's like you, he gets along. I'm serious about this. I want to get away from here and the only way is to have plenty of money. Don't think about Callahan, think about us. This is just the first time. It'll be better the next time and the next and—"

"I still have to think it over. I gave my word."

Laurie pulled away from me. "Don't take too long. You can't give me away because nobody would believe you. I had to say that. I like you *très* much, Saddler. I wish I didn't have to leave. I'll think about you in bed. I will, all night, I will. I may have to pleasure myself to ease the tension."

"Why not," I said.

FOUR

I *was sitting in the rocker on the jail porch and wonder-*
ing how much loyalty I owed Johnny Callahan when
three men rode in behind a skinny man driving a
buckboard. There was something about the four of them
that made me forget all about removing Laurie
McLandress's inheritance from the bank.

The skinny gent in the rig touched his derby hat as he
drove by, and I acknowledged it in a manner befitting a
dedicated young lawman. There was something familiar
about this mannerly gent, but it didn't strike me who he
was until he tossed the reins to one of his companions
and climbed down stiffly in front of the hotel. Earl
Danziger, that's who he was, and a bigger conniver never
drew breath. Everybody called him Earl, friends and
enemies, and he had plenty of both. At some point a
newspaper wag had written that Earl Danziger talked out
of the four sides of his mouth. That about summed him
up. Danziger wasn't just a politician, Danziger was
anything that paid money. Danziger didn't steal with a

gun. He didn't have to. By itself his mouth was a deadly weapon, and it sure was a big one. I knew Danziger because he was from Texas, all over Texas, and maybe he'd even been born there.

At one time, every tree in Texas seemed to have a campaign picture of Earl Danziger nailed to it. Every tree, every barn, every railroad depot, stage station and ferry crossing had its picture of oily Earl. He got to be a state senator but got stuck there, and when there was a railroad scandal, instead of running for cover, Earl ran for governor. Brash was one of the less offensive words often used to describe the Poor Man's Friend, as he liked to be called. Most of the other names are too dirty to repeat. Earl was a briber, a go-between, a toady of the railroad moguls until he got caught with his hand in the honey bucket. He had two cracks at the governship and almost made it the second time around. If all it took was bribery, then Earl should have been Governor of Texas. Not so oddly, the voters liked him even while they were turning him down for the highest office in the state. Earl was a showman, a snake oil salesman who always provided good entertainment. When he failed to get elected he ran his own candidates and had some success. Then he made a fatal mistake, he elected an honest man who turned on him, denouncing him as a crook and a double-dyed villain. It got so hot in Austin that old Earl decided that maybe it was time to move on. Now he was here and he had company, the kind of company I don't like.

Whatever it was, Danziger's business must have been fairly important because ten minutes hadn't passed before he came out of the hotel, climbed in the buckboard, and took the road heading north with the three hardcases trailing behind. On the way out he doffed his hat to McLandress, standing on the sidewalk outside the bank. I went over to the hotel to make sure I wasn't mistaken. I wasn't. There was his name in a big round scrawl, showy as the man himself.

The clerk seemed to know who he was and that surprised me. "Where you been, Deputy?" the clerk said, appalled by my ignorance. "Mr. Danziger is just one of the biggest men in the Territory. Business, politics, everything. Told me to call him Earl right off. That's the kind of man he is, plain as an old shoe. Now I wonder what he's doing here. Some big deal, most likely."

"Where was he headed in such a hurry?" I asked, hoping I wouldn't get an answer I wouldn't like.

I got it after I persuaded the clerk, still shaken by his brush with the great man, that it was all right to tell an officer of the law.

"He asked me how to get to the Flannery place," the clerk said. "I thought that was kind of unusual but these big men never explain things. Never explain, never apologize, that's how these rich men get rich."

"That's all he said?"

"Mr. Danziger didn't say that. I didn't say he said it. I said he asked where the Flannery place was." The clerk smirked, the only way he could get back at me for asking questions. "Why don't you ask him yourself. That's not to say you'll get an answer. And don't ask me when he'll be coming back. Mr. Danziger didn't take me into his confidence."

I didn't have to ask where the Flannery place was located because I already knew. I had been asking about Kate Flannery in a careful way. I wanted to know what there was to know about her. So far all I knew, apart from Casey's gossip, was that she came from a big family of the wildest Irish rednecks in Arizona. Nobody in town had a good word for them, though I couldn't pin down what it was they had done. They kept to themselves, made no attempt to be neighborly, took no part in the life of the town. They bought nothing they couldn't make or raise on their own land: lumber, whiskey, iron work, bullets, preserved goods. They had fenced their land with barbwire hung with TRESPASSERS WILL BE SHOT signs. And that's where Earl Danziger, the man who never risked his own skin, was going. I thought I knew why, but there was nothing to do but wait.

I went to a four-stool eating place down the street run by a gabby old geezer with a stiff leg. While he was frying up some ham and eggs, I sounded him out on the Flannerys. It was hard to get him interested; all he wanted to do was gab about Earl Danziger and what he was doing in Dragoon Wells. For some reason he didn't like Danziger. I didn't ask him the reason.

"The Flannerys, they're half wild, nobody's got any use for them," the old gent said, turning the ham, then setting out a plate and hardware for me. "Old Con Flannery come here from Ireland about thirty years ago, maybe a bit more. Him and his five brothers was in the War, the Union side. Not a one of them got killed though I guess they was in plenty of battles. They got mustered out down South and drifted out here through Texas."

"How did they get so much land? They tell me it runs clear back into the hills."

The old man slid the ham and eggs onto my plate and pulled the coffee pot off the stove. "How did they get it? They took it, that's how they got it. During the war the country here went to wrack and ruin owing to the Apaches. A lot of folks just moved on. Some that went to war never come back. Old Con and his five hardcase brothers started putting a big place together out of the small spreads. I got to be fair to the man. He bought some of the land, but mostly he took. Took and hung on like a Boston Bull. Them Irish is a fierce bunch of wild men, afraid of nothing. Whipped the Apaches till they was afraid to show their dirty face in these parts. I guess the Flannerys did that. Be a liar to say they didn't."

The eggs were fried too hard but I was hungry after my night with Laurie. "Then what do people have against them? So far nobody I've talked to has accused them of anything but being independent."

"Well, that's it—independent," the old man said. "They're too god-blasted independent. It's like the rest of us was just a bunch of trash. Who the hell are they to be so independent, a gang of half-wild potato-eating clodhoppers that probably didn't have a pair of boots till they went in the army. You think one of them'd walk in here and order a good meal like you just done? Not a chance. Don't spend a cent more than they can help. It's not like they's poor anymore, far from it."

"How many of them are there?" I figured that Danziger and his hardcases couldn't be far from the Flannery barbwire by now. "You make it sound like there's a separate nation out there."

"Too many for my money," the old man complained. "I don't know how many. Damned if they know themselves. Con and the four brothers all got married, had any number of sons and daughters, a powerful lot of sons. The sons are mostly growed and some of them has sons. If you're asking how many men out there can shoot a gun I would say probably twenty, give or take a few."

When that was out of the way I still had to wait. So I went back to the jail and cleaned guns that didn't need cleaning. The kid Calvin was cleaning the place and got in my way until I told him it was clean enough. He didn't like that and I told him he could dust and sweep twice as hard when Johnny got back. I whiled away the time by reading old wanted posters. A few faces were dead and I put them in the stove. Not much else happened.

Two hours later I suffered a disappointment when I heard Danziger and his boys coming back. I'd been hoping that Con Flannery and his Irishmen had dropped them in their tracks. When I got to the door I saw one of the hard cases was missing. So was Danziger's hat. They didn't come in as jaunty as they went out. It was a reasonable assumption that the missing man was dead. It was none of my business what he was; beyond the town limits killing was the county sheriff's concern.

I wondered if Danziger would come to me. Maybe he would. I did nothing but set a chair where I could watch the hotel through the window. Two boys from the livery stable came to take away the buckboard and the horses. The town dragged on through another dull day.

I was down to the stub of my second cigar when there was shouting down the street. It was trouble, the real start of the trouble. I went outside and a farmer with a chin beard was driving a wagon with a saddle horse tied to the tailgate. I went down to see what the farmer was hauling. I had a good idea what it was. The farmer halted the wagon in front of the jail and there was a dead man in the back of it. Danziger's missing gunman.

"Got something for you, Deputy," the farmer said in the unemotional way of farmers. "Found this man dragging from a stirrup a long way out. Dead as a nail before I found him. You'd be wanting to claim the body, I'd say. The dragging didn't kill him."

The farmer was right. There was a small hole in his forehead that must have killed him instantly. Then the horse spooked and dragged him.

"Never seen him before," the farmer said. "You know who he is?"

"Where did you find him?" I asked. "Was it out by the Flannery place?"

The farmer looked scared, no longer eager to be a part of it. "I didn't say the Flannerys had anything to do with this. Don't you go saying I did."

"Calm down, granger," I said. "You said on the road. The road is a public place. I'm just asking was it out by the Flannery place?"

"Close enough," he said cautiously. "Not too far from the main gate. Will you be wanting me for anything else? My name is Eben Linkhorn, everybody knows me."

I dragged the dead man out by the ankles and dumped him in the street and rolled him on his face. The back of his head was blown away. The farmer turned his team and drove off, and I dragged the body up on the porch and covered it with a blanket from the cells. People crowded around asking questions, but all the excitement wasn't enough to bring Danziger and his boys out of the hotel. While I was tucking in the dead man, I took a gander at the hotel door. The only one in it was the clerk.

Calvin showed up and I asked him if the town had an undertaker. "Not anymore," he said. "The lumber man buries them now."

"Go fetch him," I said. "Tell him to take this thing out of here. No burying till I say so. The county sheriff may want to hold an inquest. Get it straight, Calvin, no funeral just yet."

The boy bobbed his head and hurried away and I went over to the hotel. No one was in the lobby except the clerk. "What's going on, Deputy? That dead man was with Mr. Danziger this morning. You here to tell Mr. Danziger? He's in the Governor's Suite. Second floor, end of the hall."

I found the door and knocked on it. One of the hard cases opened it a few inches and grunted. I took that to be a question. The hard case had one hand on his gun. Cigar smoke seeped out through the crack in the door.

"I want to see Danziger," I said.

The hard case didn't budge. I guess he thought he had to act tough in front of his boss, or maybe he needed the practice. Hard cases are better actors than actors.

"We call him *Mister* Danziger. What do you want?" Inside I heard the creak of someone getting on or off a bed.

You get tired of hard cases who try to look and dress the part. The real badmen don't have to bother. One of the deadliest killers I ever knew was a man in his fifties who looked like a mining engineer.

"My name is Saddler, I'm the law," I said. "Open the door or you'll be wearing it in a minute."

Then Danziger's voice called out from inside, "Open up, Lattigo. There's no call for any of that."

I went in and Danziger was stretched out on the bed, a long thin cigar tilting skyward from his loose, liver-colored lips. The other hard case was over by the window, hand on gun, looking my way. Bottles and glasses were in a polished wood box that hinged down in front, and when closed it could be carried by a handle. It was a big room with other rooms running off it. It was fancy but faded, and it looked like the governor hadn't been there lately.

Danziger had taken off his elastic sided shoes and was resting his feet on a pillow. When he held up his glass, the hard case by the window came over and filled it. Danziger watched me from the bed. "Something I can do for you, Deputy?"

"You're missing a man," I said.

"Thanks for telling me. You got anything else to tell me, seeing you're here."

Danziger had the hambone politician's flapping mouth. He didn't seem to listen to everything he said. I know that sounds funny, but maybe if you've been in so many of the same situations you just use the words you've used before. His words straggled out as if he found it hard to keep his mind on the proceedings. Everything he said had a tired tone, sort of sneering. I could see why the voters had shied away from him. The voters may be dumb, but they do show occasional good sense.

Danziger smiled encouragement. "I know you have something else to tell me. What is it?"

"Your man was brought in dead, a farmer found him shot," I said. "I sent the body over to the undertaker's. Will you be paying for the funeral, or will it go on the county?"

Danziger sipped his whiskey. "That's shocking news," he said. "Poor Andy. Of course, you know, I wasn't all that well acquainted with him. How about you boys? By the way, Deputy, I'd like you to meet Billy Rice and Harry Lattigo."

I knew that Billy Rice was a Texas gunman with a bad name in Brownsville and other places. I would have figured him to be older, but maybe he started young. He must have because he wasn't 30 yet. He was the one who poured Danziger's whiskey. He was dark haired and pale faced and wore dark clothes. He carried a short-barreled Sheriff's Model Colt .45 in a stiff holster. I think he was closer to his boss than the other gunman, a runt with mad-dog gray eyes and a down-home accent.

Rice nodded and Lattigo didn't do anything but stare. He hadn't forgiven me for our little chat at the door. Rice would be faster, that was pretty plain, which is not to say that Lattigo wasn't fast himself. But if it came to shooting, Rice would have to be shot first.

"How did it happen?" I asked Danziger.

He faked surprise. "You tell me, Deputy. Harmon, that's the dead man, decided he wanted to take a look at the country. We came on back and here we are. Who do you suppose could have shot him?"

"How about the Flannerys?"

"Never heard of them," Danziger said. "You boys ever hear that name?"

Rice and Lattigo said no. "I don't know what to tell you," Danziger said. "My guess is poor Harmon was done in by road agents, something like that."

"Don't take it so hard," I said.

"I said I was deeply shocked, that'll have to do," Danziger said.

"Maybe it will."

"Hey, Deputy," Lattigo cut in. "You're coming down kind of heavy for what you are. That's Mr. Earl Danziger you're talking to."

"I know who he is."

"Wait a minute, hold on there!" Danziger said without getting off the bed. He finished off the whiskey and handed the glass to Rice. "What's eating on you, Deputy? You come in here with a chip as big as a railroad tie and start throwing your weight around. You got something against my men? Against me? If we've met before I don't recall it. Did I do you some wrong? You asked questions and you got answers. You don't like the answers, should I make up new ones? We don't know these Flannerys. All right, Harmon wandered off and got shot. Are you hinting we killed him? I think not, sir. You're the law—go catch Harmon's killer."

"Somebody stole your hat, maybe I can catch him at the same time." I thought that would get under his thick skin. It did.

Danziger swung his legs off the bed and sat up. Rice gave him a fresh cigar and a light. "Don't push it too hard, Deputy," Danziger warned, clouding up the room. "You have a lot to learn in the way of politeness, so why don't you save the tough talk for the Saturday night drunks. I'm a plain man, get along with everybody, try best I can. If somebody bothers me I tell them what I'm telling you: don't crowd me. I make a good friend and a bad enemy. Think about it, my friend."

Danziger lay down again and put his hands behind his head, the cigar tilted in his flabby mouth. Eyes closed as if he couldn't bear to see any more of the world's foolishness, he drawled out, "Harry, do a tired old man a favor. Go downstairs and find me something to eat. Then stop by the church and say a prayer for Harmon."

They were laughing when I left.

FIVE

Calvin was watching them load the dead man into a spring wagon when I got back to the jail. He wanted to know if he should dash out to Johnny's ranch to tell him about the killing and the strangers in town.

"You like the marshal, don't you?" I asked him.

"You bet," he said proudly. "Me and the marshal has been working together since my folks died four years ago. We get along good."

"Then stay away from him just now," I said. "He's got to let those legs heal up and that won't happen if he starts bumping about in that wheelchair. If something real bad happens, I'll tell you to go. Watch the jail till I get back. I'm going out to the Flannery place."

That shook him up. "Gosh!" he said.

It took about two hours to get to the start of their property, a swing gate in a barbwire fence that ran away into the distance on both sides. It was true what Casey said: they owned a powerful sight of land. It went all the way back to distant hills. On the gate was one of the

46

TRESPASSERS WILL BE SHOT signs, but nobody shot at me as I opened it. I guess the sign and their reputation for pugnacity were enough. My rights as a lawman ended the instant I crossed the town line; then I was just another trespasser. Even so, I hoped the badge would have some meaning to them. It was too bad they weren't nice law-abiding Germans instead of wild Irishmen. In this matter of shooting trespassers, the law was on their side. Good sense told me to turn back. I ignored my own advice and went ahead.

A good road started at the gate and went straight back through trees and a scatter of low hills. I got to the hills and through them without getting any extra holes in me. Past the hills was a wide, well-grassed valley with the silver slash of a small river in the middle of it. I don't know how many cows were down there—maybe 3,000—and I figured that was just part of the herd. It was hot and quiet in the long valley, with no sign of a house until the road tipped up and went down again into another wide stretch of country. Then I saw a big sprawl of houses and buildings far off on the other side of a big pond that had been made by damming a creek. From where I was it looked like a town instead of a ranch. Smoke spiraled up into the hard blue sky and the screech of a sawmill was carried by the hot wind. In the sunlight the houses and buildings were a glaring white.

I started down the hill, a rifle cracked and somebody far away rang a bell. The bell went on ringing like a church calling the godly to prayer on Sunday morning. You couldn't have counted to 45 before men on horses, a lot of men and horses, were heading my way. I kept on going until a big-caliber rifle splintered rock in the road a few feet in front of me.

I expected them to come whooping but they rode in silence, all carrying rifles. Others, alerted by the bell, still clanging, rode in from both sides of the road. It was too late to run. If I did I'd be lifted out of the saddle by bullets. They got to me and some galloped past, heading

47

for the main gate, as if to repel an invasion. They seemed to have a plan worked out in case of an attack.

The big man with the shaggy gray hair had to be Con Flannery. Cornelius Flannery, to give him his full name, had three inches and 50 pounds on me, a great brute of a man, straight backed for his age, somewhere in his late fifties. Three of the other men had the same height and powerful build, the same wide, sun-seamed faces. In town the people called Flannery "Old Con"; there was nothing old about him except his age. He sat atop a big claybank as lithe as an Indian and the good-looking Creedmore Sharps was small in his huge, work-hardened hands.

"Take his guns," Flannery ordered in a sandpapery voice that still had some Irish left in it. A younger version of the old man snatched my Winchester from the boot and got my beltgun. Every man there was mounted well, no nags for this mean-spirited bunch.

"You must be a fool," Flannery said. "It's a good thing for you you came in straight and in broad day. That's not to say you're going to ride out as cool as you came in. Mister, can I ask you a question? What do you think those signs are for?"

"I'm not trespassing," I said. "I came here to see Con Flannery. Is that you?"

"That's who I am. We're all Flannerys here, no strangers. You're a stranger. I don't know what you want, don't want to know. I don't talk to people less I have to do, and, Mister, I don't have to talk to you. Now turn that horse and get out before you get shot."

The young Flannery who took my guns had been looking me over. "Shoot him anyway, Con. He's up to something. This is Callahan's new saddletramp."

"Be off now," Con Flannery said to me. "You see how it is. The boys will ride with you. You must be lucky. You hear what I just said."

"I still want to talk to you."

"You don't listen, do you?"

"It's as important to you as it is to me."

"Nothing that you have to say is important to me, *Saddler*."

Word got around fast. They knew I worked for Johnny and they knew my name. "A man got killed this morning but that's not why I'm here, Mr. Flannery. If you shot a trespasser that's your business."

"Sure," Flannery said. "It's legal. I don't need you to tell me that. One more time I'll tell you—get out."

I said no and the Creedmore came up and pointed at me. It's a dandy, that Creedmore Sharps. Even going in, a bullet from a Creedmore makes a big hole. When it goes out it takes your spine with it. Flannery was right, I was a fool.

"Come along then," Flannery said at last. "It's bad luck to kill an idiot. That's what you are, Saddler. You had your chance and didn't take it. If I don't like what you have to say, it'll go hard on you."

"Fair enough," I said.

"Don't be so agreeable," Flannery growled. "You won't like it a bit."

The road ran straight down to the pond and around it to the other side. Cows grazed on the good grass, fat and slow moving. Far back were hills, beyond that mountains. Reeds grew along the side of the pond and cows stood knee-deep in the shore muck drinking water. For a while I couldn't see the main ranch because of the windbreak of trees. Then we were through the trees and I was looking at the best spread I'd seen for many a day. The big house was long and low with a Texas breezeway in the middle. Horses moved about in a long corral; a water tower and a red barn stood back from the house. In the distance there were other houses and barns. Flowers grew in beds in front of the house and under a shade tree, heavy and green, a swing creaked in the wind.

I got down and they took my horse and Flannery pointed me into the house. A trim gray-haired woman of Flannery's age looked at me from the breezeway before she went away. I didn't see Kate Flannery, but the door of the barn was open and the shiny black buggy was inside. Flannery didn't miss the look I gave it.

Inside, the main room of the house was long, dark and cool after the sun. It was sensible rather than fancy, no grand piano, no oil paintings, things favored by some ranchers who got rich. The floor was scrubbed white, bleached by strong soap, and sanded with fine white sand. Over the high stone fireplace hung an old regimental flag and the Stars and Stripes, a heavy saber in the old cavalry style, and a Navy Colt. Solid wood-and-leather chairs lined a dark dining room table on both sides. We sat at the table and Flannery said, "Get on with it."

I never saw a man more disinclined to help the law of the land. Con Flannery had a way of making everything he said sound final, like Moses setting the Israelites straight on this and that. That seemed to work with his kin, and they obeyed him without question, but I wasn't sure how far it would go with Earl Danziger and, the real threat, Peyton Ballard. It got very quiet in the big room.

"I know I'm not the law in the county," I said. He didn't comment on that. "But I'm the law in Dragoon Wells and that's where Danziger and his two gunmen are. This morning Danziger rode out this way with three men, came back with two. The third was brought in dead by a farmer."

"Make your point," Flannery said, looking at the reflection of his hands in the polished tabletop.

"I think Danziger came out here to say something you didn't like. Maybe he figured he could talk tough because he had the three gunslingers to back his play. He was wrong. You told him where to go and one of the hard-cases got shot when he reached. You could have killed all of them, but you let them go. Maybe that was a mistake, letting them go."

Flannery kept his hands still. "That a fact now?" he said. "It could have happened that way. This Danziger, what would he be wanting with me? You better answer that the politest way you know how. I do mean that."

I knew I could kill Flannery if he got mad enough to pull a gun on me. Then I could kill a few more Flannerys before they cut me down. There was no doubt about what the outcome of the fight would be. I'd be dead.

"Your daughter came back here last night," I said. Flannery's eyes didn't budge from mine. "I saw her myself on her way through town. I was told her name. It's hard to say what I have to say next, Mr. Flannery."

Flannery's voice was quiet, almost mild. "I'll decide how hard to take it, Saddler. What about my daughter?"

For an instant, I heard the rustle of silk in one of the dark doorways that led off the main room, and I knew she was there, listening. I don't know if Flannery heard it.

"They say your daughter is married to a man named Peyton Ballard, a rancher in Sonora."

Flannery found some grim humor in my delicate attempt not to hurt his feelings and get myself killed. "You can describe him better than that. Say he's a butcher and a renegade who's been trying to act like a gentleman. That's what he is, for all his money and influence."

Anyway, he hadn't denied it, so I guess the story was true. I said, "The way I see it, Danziger came here to persuade your daughter to go back to her husband. Ballard can't come himself or they'd hang him. So he sent Danziger as the go-between. Danziger brought along the three gunmen to give him confidence. One of them got shot, the rest ran. They looked like they'd been running when they got back to town."

"You tell a good story," Flannery said. "But you still haven't made your point, if there is a point. Is there?"

"Did it happen the way I just said, Mr. Flannery?" I asked. "Did Danziger come here to try to take your daughter?"

"If he did come, what has it got to do with you?"

"Meaning I'm not county law."

"The law's got nothing to do with it, county or not."

"If there's killing, the law has to get into it, Mr. Flannery."

What I said didn't bother him. "Any trouble comes up can be handled by us. That means me. You saw my brothers and the rest of our people just now. You think they're the kind to get scared because a few saloon thugs come here with their tied-down guns. We don't tie our guns down, Deputy, we shoot them. Another thing, you didn't see all of us. There's a few more up in the hills."

I had to admit that the Flannerys looked formidable enough. They could handle a lot more than Danziger and his two gunmen. But how much was a lot? Using Ballard's money, Danziger could buy all the gunmen he needed, more than he needed. This wasn't far from the border—what if Ballard decided to come himself? Word was that he had his politician friends scheming to get him a pardon, the only reason why he was trying to get his woman back the easy way. He could kiss the pardon goodbye if he came north of the border with his Sonora pistoleros. That was where the real threat lay, not in Danziger and his American gunmen. But they'd be bad enough, if they came in force, and I felt sure they would come, if something wasn't done about it. So far only one man had died; if the gunmen came, bodies would be falling like autumn leaves. Even so, Ballard was the man on my mind. Down where he was he could recruit the most dangerous men in the world, Mexican pistoleros. Men so mean, so empty of human feeling, that they'd kill a child for a dollar and a drink. They prowled the border country like wolves, half starved in their dirty though fancy clothes, their only trade murder for hire, and Peyton Ballard had the money to pay them all.

"You're thinking we can't take care of ourselves," Flannery said, staring hard at my expressionless face. "This talk is all just suppose. I'm not saying I have a daughter, I'm not saying she's here."

"You were in the war," I said. "What was the real

reason the Union beat the Rebs?"

"More men. Ah now, is that what you're thinking? You think they'd go to that much trouble?"

"Ballard's done worse in his time. Time doesn't change a man. Often he gets meaner than he was. If Danziger fails here, then Ballard will come. He'll weigh the pardon against the rest of it and decide the hell with it. You won't be able to handle him, Mr. Flannery. That's my answer. The town won't be able to handle him."

"Who in hell cares about the town?"

"I don't much, still they're people. What you need is help. I'd like to help any way I can."

I meant what I said, but the Irishman wasn't buying my wares. He raised his hand to stop me from saying anything more. "You've been telling me about Danziger, nothing I didn't know. The man's a public disgrace. Ballard doesn't need any explaining to me. I was a grown man before you were born, Saddler, so what Ballard was and is isn't news to me. But what about you? What do I know about you? Yesterday you weren't here and now you are. It's said that Callahan will vouch for you. That cuts no ice with me, more than the other way round. It could be that you didn't come to Dragoon Wells by chance."

"That's how it happened," I said, understanding his suspicion. A lot of people were suspicious about the way I came there.

"Nobody's calling you a liar, but you see my side of it. You could be working for Ballard yourself. You got here last night, Danziger got here this morning. All that could be more than a coincidence."

"Where does Callahan fit into this? Did Ballard send word to get his legs broken so I could take over?" I knew I had him there.

His smile had all the warmth of a judge's heart. "Maybe Callahan didn't plan to break his legs. That doesn't mean he didn't know you were coming. Maybe you and Callahan are part of it, maybe just you. I've got no reason to trust you, Saddler."

"What do you think I'm doing in Dragoon Wells?"

"For one thing, you're talking to me, something Danziger didn't get to do. You could be here to tell me what a bad man Peyton Ballard is so I won't get in his way. Answer me a question. When were you ever a lawman?"

Lying wouldn't get me anywhere with this hard-eyed man. "Never," I said. "This is my first time. That's not to say I won't do what I'm paid for."

"You have the look of a drifter," Flannery went on. "Nothing wrong with that by itself. I figure you for a gambler, a poker player. You play hard to win but you know how to lose. You lost here."

"What makes you say that, Mr. Flannery?"

"You bluffed your way in here, but a bluff can be called. I'm calling you, Saddler. Find yourself another game. This game is private, a family party you got no part in. Makes no difference to me if you're looking out for yourself or for Ballard. Here we are and here we stay. If Ballard comes here, here he'll be buried. That plain enough for you? You might tell that to Danziger so he can pass it along."

"I think he knows it by now."

"Pass along something else while you're at it," Flannery said. "A small bit of history. When me and my brothers came here there was nothing. During the war this was Secesh country, still is, a lot of it. We'd been good loyal soldiers but that didn't put meat on the table. We were Union men and Irish bogtrotters too, and that made us less welcome than we were. If the people had been friendly we'd have paid them in kind. They weren't friendly—anything but. What you probably didn't hear is they tried to run us out and that, my friend, was a terrible mistake. We don't own a blade of grass we didn't work for. Now we're rich—fools hate that word—so we don't have to be friendly. Leave us be, is all we ask. We fought whites and Indians and beat them and we'll do the same for Ballard's greasers."

Once again I heard the rustle of the silk dress in the darkened hallway. I wondered what she thought of all this. There had been a big row with the old man before she ran off and married Ballard. It wouldn't be hard to quarrel with Con Flannery. There are some men who just know that God has given them the right to tell people what to do. Con Flannery was one of them, as bullheaded a man as ever roared out an order.

"It won't be any kind of fair fight. Your people may fight like wildcats, but there aren't enough of them," I said. "And from what I hear, you can't expect much help from the county sheriff. Don't you have any friends at all that will back you? You can't stand up to them by yourself."

Flannery looked around the big solid house and seemed to get reassurance. "My family are my friends, all I need. We'll make do, we always have. Everything in life is a gamble and so is this. You'd best go along now. Don't come back here—ever!"

"You mean I don't get shot?"

"Don't come back, I said. You may be all right, Saddler, but it's still none of your business. If you came out of real concern I appreciate it. But I'll say it again—don't come back."

I had an escort all the way to the gate.

SIX

When I got back to Dragoon Wells it was getting dark, and not being Saturday night, it was quiet. The brightest light was in Casey's saloon; the saloon was quiet like the town. The old geezer who ran the restaurant was closing up, but he unbolted the door when he saw me.

"Treat the customers right and they come back," he said. He thought opening for me entitled him to questions. I turned the questions aside and told him to fry up a big steak and charge it to Callahan.

"No offense, you better pay me. Callahan won't," he said.

I put money on the counter and asked how things had been going. There was no need to say what things because the whole town was still buzzing with talk of Kate Flannery having something to do with the dead man. It was suppertime for the town and I wondered what Laurie was doing. I knew I wouldn't throw her out of bed if she came over later after the town blew out the lights.

The door of the restaurant was closed and bolted; the place was empty except for us, yet the old man lowered his voice and looked around before he spoke. "One of them sidekicks of Danziger come over here to get food about the time you left. You'd think he was in some city, the way he bitched about my cooking. I guess they ate it all right. Later he come over for more."

The steak wasn't bad and I was hungry. "Then they stayed in the hotel?"

"One man didn't, he rode out about an hour after you left. Took the road he came in on, in a terrible hurry. Where do you suppose he went to?"

I knew as much as he did, which was nothing. After I finished the steak I went over to the hotel and got upstairs without waking the clerk. I think that man needed to get a lot of sleep. Lattigo opened the door and was as glad to see me as the first time. But there was no tough talk, and I was glad of that. It hadn't been such a good day and I was ready to break his teeth with my gun barrel.

"Deputy's here again," he said over his shoulder. Danziger told him to let me in. He sounded a bit drunk.

"What's it this time?" he asked looking at his hat. I guess he was thinking the hole in the hat could have been in his head.

I spun the hat onto the bed and it landed by his feet. "You forgot that when you were out to the Flannery place."

Danziger nudged the hat onto the floor, saying, "That can't be my hat, Deputy, got a hole in it." He laughed but Lattigo didn't.

The window was closed though it was a warm evening and the room stank of cigar smoke. Nothing had changed except that Danziger was more droopy eyed than usual. Still on the bed, a glass in his hand, he didn't look as casual as he sounded. His crinkly ginger hair was mussed and he combed it back with his fingers. Then he fixed his blue ribbon tie.

57

"But thanks for thinking of me," he said. "Hope you didn't go to much trouble getting it. By the way, how about a drink? We got off on the wrong foot this morning."

I'll say this for Danziger. He drank good whiskey. All his other good points escaped me. The slack-mouth son of a bitch pointed to his glass and Lattigo filled it. I got a full one too.

"To your good health, sir," Danziger toasted me.

"Mrs. Ballard sends her regards," I said, knocking back the whiskey.

"Hey, wait a minute, slow down there," Danziger said, putting his bare feet on the floor. "Don't just drink and run, Deputy. And don't tell me my whiskey isn't good—it's the best." I knew he was talking to give himself time to think. "What was that woman's name you just said?"

"Kate Flannery Ballard," I said. "Red hair, green eyes, nice figure."

"Yeah," Danziger said appreciatively though he was surely past the age when he could do anything active to a woman. If old Earl got a bone on he would need a lot of help. But there was fond remembrance in his drawling voice.

He looked up at me, still grinning. "You a friend of Kate?"

"From way back."

"You're a liar," Danziger said mildly, still grinning. "You may know what she looks like; that's all you know. Can't say I blame you for wanting to claim her friendship. You can't know her, Deputy. You haven't been in town much longer than we have. Fess up now."

"I like what I saw of her," I said.

Danziger watched me carefully, trying to size me up. He was a big noise in the Territory but he had corns and bunions like any old man. "That kind of talk could get you in trouble if it got back to the wrong man," he said. "Why don't you just forget about Kate. Be smart, do that."

The bluff was working, but I still didn't know where I was going. "I'd find that hard to do. I ha e a soft spot for ladies in distress, any kind of trouble. Apart from personal feelings, it's part of my job to look out for the taxpayers."

Danziger sidetracked for a while. He tried to sound casual, even friendly, but I knew his crooked brain was working hard to figure out what I wanted. I figured he would try the soft talk first, then rush in with the threats if that didn't work. He pulled his rubbery lips back in what he hoped would pass for a smile.

"This isn't much of a job you got here, is it?" he remarked, man to man, not offensive.

"I like the town and the pay isn't bad," I said. Out at the ranch Kate would be having supper or fighting with her father. I hoped she'd appreciate what I was trying to do for her, whatever it was.

"So you say," Danziger said. "But I hear it's just temporary till the marshal is walking again. You'll be looking for other work when he is. How'd you like to come to work for me?"

"Doing what?"

"What any man does that works for another man: what he's told. That's what Harry and Billy do. Job pays just fine, not that much to do. People don't bother me too much after I explain things to them. Harry and Billy back up my explanations. You could get used to it, Deputy."

I grinned at Lattigo. "I don't like to go about scaring the people. Besides, some of the little old ladies are pretty tough."

"Later for you," Lattigo said, his eyes measuring me for a coffin.

"You got enough nerve, that's for sure," Danziger said, smacking his lips over the whiskey. He must have been born poor, the way he enjoyed things so hard. "There's plenty of things you can do. Maybe it's just as well you don't work with Lattigo. You could get along with Rice, never Lattigo. I'd be short a man in no time."

"It wouldn't be me," Lattigo said.

"Hush up," Danziger said. "These days I hang out in Tucson, a nice coming little city. Climate couldn't be better, not too much disorganized crookery. I could fix you up with a job as one of the territorial attorney's deputies. Pay's good because it's a political job. Not to mention the travel money and the fees. A smart man like you could advance himself in no time. How do you feel about that?"

"I'm thinking," I said.

Danziger studied the sticky end of his cigar. "It's not like you'd have to work. Only a fool works when he doesn't have to. That's the sweet thing about this job, no work. Yes sir, I'd say you'd make a fine territorial deputy."

I helped myself to more whiskey, and Danziger took that as a good sign. "Drink up, plenty more. How's Callahan?"

"Getting along good," I said. "You don't know him?"

"I know of him," Danziger said. "Like the rest of the people I thought he was dead. Then I heard he just lost his nerve, the reason he stayed on here."

Maybe Danziger was right about Johnny. I'd been wondering why he'd bury himself in a backwater like Dragoon Wells. It seemed to me that he had talked too much about the soft life of a small town lawman, all the money he was making, as if he wanted to convince himself more than he wanted to convince me. Or it could be that Danziger was hinting that I couldn't depend on Johnny, if it came to a showdown. It wasn't much of a threat. Johnny would be in bed, in a wheelchair or on crutches for a month or six weeks.

"Maybe I should be talking to Callahan instead of you," Danziger said. "Seeing as you just work for the man."

"I'm the boss right now," I said. "You better go on talking to me."

"Callahan could fire you, isn't that a fact?"

"He could. That doesn't say I'd go."

Danziger laughed a wheezy laugh, trying to get it out of his bony chest. "Damnedest lawman I ever saw. The town hires Callahan to tame the bullies, then when it's done he won't give back the badge. Now Callahan hires you and you say you won't go if you're fired. A lawless lawman, that's what you are."

So he wouldn't miss the point, I said, "I won't let the law get in the way of what I want to do."

"Which is?"

"Look out for the Flannery girl."

"I thought we were talking about your new job in Tucson. Suddenly we're back to what's none of your business."

"It's hard to stay away from it."

Danziger sighed, a grand strategist bothered by a lance corporal. "All right then, there it is. You know who Peyton Ballard is? All right, you do, who doesn't? I want to establish that fact." Danziger was like a lawyer laying a foundation, as they say. I guess he was some kind of lawyer. "It's important that you realize the sort of a man Peyton Ballard is. Don't talk, listen. On the face of it, it's a simple thing that happens every day and doesn't call for much talk. Mr. and Mrs. Ballard had a disagreement, a fight, and she lit out from home. Now she's back where she started only a lot richer than when she left. She didn't just take her personal things but a satchelful of gold pieces, Mexican Double Eagles, folding money, American, and a mess of jewelry. How much in all? More than fifty thousand, could be closer to sixty. The money is just part of it, but it is a big part of it. Ballard wants his wife back and he wants her with the money. To him it's one and the same thing."

"And she doesn't want to go," I said.

"That's what she thinks," Danziger said. "Being a woman, she doesn't know her own mind. Sir, she left a veritable paradise to come back here. In Sonora she lived in a hacienda so close to a castle it didn't make any difference. Servants to wait on her hand and foot. The finest clothes. . . ."

Danziger talked on, enjoying his own windy statements. I was thinking about Peyton Ballard. As Danziger said, everybody knew who he was, hero or villain, depending on which side you favored in the Civil War. Even so, there were plenty of good old Rebels who despised him for what he was, what he had done. It wasn't the bank robbing and train wrecking that bothered them so much. For a time, right after the war, that sort of thing had been a national sport, like this new baseball. Ballard might have had his crimes forgiven if he hadn't burned out a townful of peaceful Germans in South Texas.

The men had fought for the Union and were back working their farms when Ballard and his Reb diehards swooped down on them in the dark, burning the town, shooting every man over the age of 14. That, at last, was the lump that couldn't be digested. It lay like lead in the belly, and it wouldn't come up or pass out the other end. Ballard knew what he had done, and knowing it, he got worse, and in the doing of it, he got rich. It took a cavalry campaign to drive him out.

"That's it in a nutshell," Danziger was saying. "Ballard wants his wife and his money, and he won't take no."

"Maybe he should come himself," I said. "Of course they'd hang him if he did. It'll take more than money to get him a pardon for killing those Germans."

"You're talking crazy, Deputy. What you're repeating is a pack of rotten lies. Sure Ballard did some wild things in his time. I'll bet you did a few. But he had nothing to do with murdering those squareheads. Fact is he's posted a standing reward of twenty thousand dollars for the apprehension of the real killers. He's not that far from catching them either. If you knew the money he's spent on detective agencies. As near as we can make out those squareheads were killed by Mexican bandits from across the river."

Danziger was getting worked up by his own words. He shook his head, saddened by the idea that people actually thought Peyton Ballard, landowner and friend of politicians, was an outlaw. "You don't think for a minute I'd be helping Peyton if any of this was true. For God's sake! Mark my words, Deputy, one of these days Peyton is going to prove his innocence."

I was watching Lattigo, not sure that he wouldn't make a try for me. Gunmen wouldn't be gunmen if they weren't a little crazy.

"That's interesting," I said. "But what happens if she keeps saying no? There's no law that says she can't leave her husband. She's not a Mormon or a slave."

Danziger considered that. "There's a law against stealing," he said. "What she took didn't belong to her. A husband's property doesn't belong to his wife and that, Deputy, is also the law. Peyton has papers to prove he owns everything she stole."

"Why doesn't he come here and make a charge against her, send her to the penitentiary? You know the answer to that as well as I do."

"I have another answer for it. You ever hear of something called extradition?"

"From here to Mexico? That doesn't sound too likely."

"Still, it could be done if one of Peyton's friends got as far as the Mexican president. President Diaz is a good friend of Uncle Sam. A lot of American capital is invested down there. Diaz could do some squeezing, as a favor. What's one woman when you're looking at big money?"

That was a new twist, one that might work. "Ballard would go that far? He'd end up owing a lot of favors, if he did. He'd have to spend more than fifty thousand to get the Mexicans to dance for him."

"You keep on missing the point no matter how hard I

63

prod you," Danziger said impatiently. "Forget about money, Peyton wants his wife back and he means to get her. I can't make that clear enough. Personally, I can't make that clear enough. The world's full of honey-fuck women with pretty faces and all you need is money to get them. No matter, it so happens that Peyton Ballard wants this one. I tell you she must be something for him to want her so bad. That's why I'm here, Deputy, to see that he gets her. Hell, it's not such a big thing, is it? Once she's back she'll see the sense of it."

"You're missing *my* point—she doesn't want to go."

"Oh Lord," Danziger said. "You keep saying that and I'm getting sick of it. She's going back, that's all there is to it. The reason I'm here is Peyton figured I could talk sense into her. If I do say so, I am known to have some powers of persuasion. Persuade, that's the word, not force. I'd hate for it to come to that."

It was time to say it, then see what happened. "That's the only way you're going to get her," I said. "You're right, I don't know her. But you're not getting her."

For once, Danziger wasn't faking his puzzlement. "I don't get it, Deputy," he said slowly, trying to be honest, which was very hard for him. "I could see it if she'd promised herself to you, if you'd stuck it in that sweet juicy crotch of hers. You haven't though, nor are you likely to. I hardly know her but I know this. You may have a big dingus on you, but it takes more than that to get Kate Flannery interested. I hear she likes a big cock, but even bigger money is what she wants. Hell, you may not even have a big enough pizzle—so why? I'd really like to know your reasoning."

Wearied by this gust of honesty, Danziger lay back on the heaped-up pillows and waited for my answer.

I said, "You're most of the reason, Danziger. Not all of it. I don't like the way you do things, with your bag of money and your gunslingers. If you don't like it you know what you can do about it." In a way, I hoped he would try to finish me, then and there. If Rice had been there I might not have been so eager. But I knew I could stop Lattigo with one shot, then do for old Earl with the next one. No doubt that wouldn't be the finish of it. Even so, Ballard might have trouble finding another go-between as slippery as Danziger.

"You'll get yours," Danziger said. "Not here though." I could tell he was nervous, knew what I was thinking.

I gave him more to think about. Why not, I was an enemy now. "If the girl wants to stay I'll see that she does. Try me and see how bad I can be. You may start the trouble here, but I'll finish it. You think because you have money and guns you can walk in here and take a woman who doesn't want to be taken. About getting her extradited to Mexico, you can try that too. You're a lawyer, you want to see what real law looks like."

Before Lattigo could blink I had the Colt out and pointing at Danziger's face. Lattigo blinked, so did Danziger. "This is the only law I care about, the only law you're going to see if you touch that girl. I'll kill you and I'll kill Ballard too, if he comes."

Danziger turned sullen, no more folksy smiles. "He will if he has to, Deputy. The door's always open should you change your mind. After it's shut, there's no way you can get in."

I holstered the Colt, still wanting to kill them. It came hard not to. It would clean up so much shit. When I think back on what happened later, it was too bad I didn't just go ahead and do it. Backing out of there, the last thing I heard from Danziger was, "No way you can win, Deputy. You don't have one chance in this world."

Maybe he was right.

SEVEN

I lay on the bed with my boots off and thought about Dougal McLandress's bad little girl. She was something to think about, that one. So saucy and clever, with a body just aching for cock. The thought of going off to Mexico City with her would cause me no pain. It wouldn't last but what the hell! Nothing lasts. But while it lasted, what a time we'd have. I've been in fine hotels in my time. I don't always sleep in jails or on the ground with a saddle for a pillow. A few weeks with Laurie McLandress would set me up for the hard life that is our lot. You bet it would.

I could see us in a swank hotel in the Avenida, that big wide boulevard in the center of the city, all flowers and palm trees, and mornings we could have breakfast with the French windows open, with the sounds and smells of the city coming through. In a hotel like that, the more money you pay, the bigger the beds. If I did it, if I went with her, we were going to need a big bed. Maybe we'd stay in bed for a week and have waiters come up with thick steaks and cold champagne. Oysters on a bed of ice. Roast duck. Cold duck. But for me, the main course would always be Laurie.

If she dragged me to theatres, maybe I'd go. Maybe I'd even leave my beltgun at home. I'd buy something with a short barrel to carry in my coat pocket. A hotel like that would have big roomy bathtubs, and we'd get in there together, roll around in the sudsy water and do all sorts of exercise. She was 19 and she knew what she got it for. Oh Lord, did she ever!

I was good and horny when there was a light tap on the door. It was after midnight and the town had gone to bed. The tap came again as I was pulling on my boots. I went to the hinged peephole with a gun in my hand and saw a boy in a big hat looking up and down the street. I couldn't see the face under the hat. But when I opened the door it wasn't a boy—it was Kate Flannery!

Her eyes were emerald in the lamplight, clear and shining. Her red hair had been tucked up under the hat; some of it had come loose. I must have gaped because she kicked the door shut with her heel and locked it before I got a chance to say anything. She wore dark blue wool pants and a leather vest over a red shirt. She should have worn a green shirt to go with her eyes. It wasn't the time or place to tell her. Saying nothing, she went straight to Callahan's desk, opened the deep drawer and took out whiskey and glasses. When I saw the second glass I knew I'd been invited to whatever it was. In my own jail.

"I want to talk to you, Saddler!" she said in a hard ringing voice. There was no Charleston finishing school in this voice. It wasn't a country voice, but a voice of her own. Maybe there was a little Irish in it, though not what you'd call soft and sentimental.

"I'm here," I said. This one would have to be put in her place. That was the first thought I had the first time I saw her in the buggy. It would take some doing. I was ready to try.

She took her whiskey and walked around with it. I sat

down and let her walk off her impatience, her anger. At the door, she spun around and stared hard at me. "What kind of man are you, Saddler? Will you help me or not?"

"Help you how? I went to see your father. He said you didn't need any help."

She downed her whiskey and refilled the glass. This was the second hard-drinking woman I'd met in Dragoon Wells. "I know you came to my father's place," she said. "I heard everything you said. You knew I heard. It's true what you said. My father doesn't know what Peyton is like. You think you do?"

"I think I do. But you know him better. Sit down and don't be so tough. It doesn't suit you."

Getting a grip on her impatience, she sat down, and the rough range clothes didn't take away a thing from her. She was taller than Laurie, but wasn't much older. There was more of her to take hold of than there was with Laurie. It was six of one, half a dozen of the other. Both women were fine with me.

"I didn't mean to sound like that," she said. "I don't want to go back to Peyton, not now, not ever. Danziger is here to bring me back. My brother killed one of Danziger's men. Because of that my father, all of them, think they can stop Peyton when he comes."

"Then you have no doubt that he'll come. You'd know better than anybody."

"There's no doubt. Peyton will come after me and he'll bring an army. You've got to do something, Saddler. I listened to you while you talked to my father. He caught something of what you are. I caught more than he did."

"What am I, Miss Flannery?" I asked.

"A gunman, a gambler, but not the usual. I think you're a very hard man, Saddler, a resourceful man. You haven't spent your life in towns like this. You know how things are done."

"Like how to stop Ballard's pistoleros?" Laurie had offered me money, but this one kept a tight purse. There

68

was no mention of the long green. I hoped that what was between her legs was just as tight. "That could get me killed, Miss Flannery."

"You can stop that polite shit, Saddler, you've been fucking me with your eyes since I walked in here. You call me Kate. I'll call you Saddler. Jim doesn't suit you."

"I'll see if I can get it changed."

"Listen, you have to help me. How bad is Callahan? Callahan would help me for old times sake."

I said no. Callahan couldn't help her unless she rode away with him in the wheelchair.

"Then it has to be you, maybe it's better that it's you," Kate said, making everything sound final, just like her father. "Callahan isn't so bad, but he doesn't have your hardness."

I don't think she meant anything by saying I was hard. But I was getting hard in another way. The thought of the money Danziger said she'd taken from Ballard crossed my mind.

Instead of money, she offered herself. I was ready to take that, for openers. The money could wait until I was ready to bring it up. "I'll do what I can," I said.

"I hope I can repay you," she said. Now that kind of talk would sound perfectly natural coming from Laurie; from Kate it had a false ring, like a lead coin. She sensed that I was grinning at her and she looked up. "You can go fuck yourself, Saddler. Don't say it. You'd rather fuck me. All right, you can. I'm not good, I'm the best. You don't believe me?"

I made the Indian peace sign. "Enough of these questions and answers at the same time. It's like there's three people in here. You and your best friend and me. Yeah, I'd like to fuck you. I mean that sincerely ... Kate."

"You'd be a fool if you didn't," Kate said, and we grinned our foxy grins. "It's a deal: do things for me and I'll do things for you. You'll like everything I do to you.

You think I'm forward, don't you?"

"Gosh no," I said. "However did you get an idea like that?"

She came up close. She had something in her hair that smelled good. "I'll show you how."

And she did. We went into Callahan's back room and into his bed. All thought of Ballard faded away as she let me take off her clothes. I like it when they don't help. I had to stoop to peel off her boy's pants, and when I got them open she gripped my head and pulled my face into her. Mom's Apple Pie! Sweet, tasty, warm! I wanted that as much as she did and she moaned as I found the right place. Her hands gripped my hair so hard that it hurt. It felt good. I widened her legs so I could get at her, give her everything, and her whole body shook as she came with quick contractions of her cunt muscles. I couldn't stand it any longer, I had to get into her. We tumbled into bed together and now it was her turn to pleasure me. I lay on my back with my bone up rock hard and throbbing, and she got on her knees between my legs and smiled at me over the top of it.

She knew how to tease, but she was enjoying it as much as I was. She licked her lips and then me. Then she took in the top and worked on that. I just about exploded when she did that, but she knew how to keep me from letting go. Compared to Kate, Laurie was just a novice with a lot to learn. Every time I was ready to let go she tightened her mouth until I was ready to beg. Then suddenly she climbed on top of me and put it inside her. We rolled over and I began to whack it into her.

There was something about her that made me want to be master. I sought to hold her down on her back and she fought me, wanting it and fighting it at the same time. We fought on, enjoying every minute of it, and I beat her. I was right about the hard doing of it, and when it was over at last and we lay together, emptied of lust and energy, she whispered, "You're a son of a bitch! No man ever did that to me!" But she smiled and asked me to get her a drink of water, then a drink of whiskey. She drank the water first.

It was quiet in the back room of the jail, with no sound but the night wind whistling. I felt sorry for Peyton Ballard. He had to be missing what I just got. I wanted more and knew I was going to get it.

"I guess you wonder why I'm so horny," she said.

"I don't wonder about it. I guess you're horny because you're a horny woman." If she could be brash, then so could I. Laurie talked about sex with a kind of horny innocence. Kate was different; there was nothing innocent about anything she said.

She didn't like my remark and raised her hand to slap my face. I caught her wrist before she could do it. Red spots burned in her cheeks, and her green eyes snapped at me. "You're a fine one to talk, you big hot-cocked bastard. You're the kind that's horny all the time. You look like you'd fuck your grandmother."

I let go her wrist. "No slapping, you hear. You slap me and I'll slap you, only harder. And let's not get nasty about my grandmother. It's not ladylike."

That stopped her. No woman, not even the toughest whore, wants to be thought of as less than a lady. "All right," she said. "Just don't be calling me a horny woman."

I didn't remind her that she started it. I didn't want to fight with her. I wanted to fuck her till dawn. After a long silence she began to stroke my shaft, the old up and down friction, until it was standing again. Then she examined it as if she'd never seen a cock before.

"My but you respond so quickly. I'll bet that big thing of yours has been in a lot of women."

"That's what it's for."

"How many would you say? Make a guess in case you don't keep score."

I lay back like an oriental potentate and she stroked me faster. It certainly was a pleasure to lay back and take my ease while she did all the work.

"I would say about a hundred," I answered after pretending to think about it. "Maybe a shade over a hundred. But a hundred I'm sure of."

She was really beating my meat now, so hard that it was beginning to hurt. I don't know why she was mad about my 100 women. The count was probably right because I've fucked every kind of woman from good-looking paroled husband killers to Nob Hill society ladies and enjoyed every one of them. Kate could hardly have had that many cocks stuck in her, but it had to be a fair number.

"My but aren't we modest?" she said, her voice heavy with sarcasm. "And did they all tell you how wonderful you were?"

"Some did, some didn't. I don't look for praise."

"Stout fella," she said, a phrase she must have picked up from some English dude. "Well, I'm going to make you come all over yourself." She stroked me harder.

I reached down to stop her. "Ease up now. I can do that for myself. Turn over. I'm going to take you from behind. Put it right through your legs and into your hotbox. I'm tired and when I am I like a cushion."

She didn't protest when I turned her over, shoved it between her thighs and straight in where I wanted to go. I like it like that. You have the woman's ass under you and it *is* like a cushion. In an instant her anger was forgotten and her ass began to move under me. It squirmed as if it were alive. I wondered if old Peyton Ballard the bandit had ever done her like that. She tried to raise up when she came, but I held her firm for my own come. She shuddered under me. I thought she was going to cry, not from sadness but from crazy, wild happiness. Old Ballard, down in Sonora, knew what he was missing. No wonder he was breaking his balls to get her back. I didn't know if he loved her. Probably he did. Loved and hated her. Love and hate would go hand in hand with this dangerous woman. I don't mean she was murderous, just dangerous. A man who didn't watch himself with her would find himself in terrible trouble. But I have a weakness for dangerous, difficult women. All I ask is that they be beautiful and willing. She was both, but she was trying to trick me. To put it plain, I wanted some of the money she took from Ballard. I was like Laurie. I wasn't greedy. I didn't want anything more than half. I was taking a bigger risk than she was. After all, I'd lose more than my pride. The worst that could happen to her would be a speedy return to the ever-loving arms of her outlaw husband. But forget about everything but the money. I wanted some.

I started off with, "I could bring in guns of my own if I had some money. Nobody here is going to back me for what Callahan can pay, what I can pay. Even if I could find them the town wouldn't give me a cent. With money to show I could send a fast message to some hardcases I know in El Paso. They could get here fast before Danziger runs out of ideas."

Kate snuggled up to me. "I wish I had some. It's too bad I don't."

"What about your father? They say he's got plenty of green."

Kate's hand moved over me. "He won't give it to me. He thinks he can handle my husband. I'm afraid there's no money."

It was time to get to it. "I thought you might have some," I said, stroking her too. "It would help if you had."

Kate sighed and felt the outlines of my face. "You aren't handsome, but you'll do," she said, adding, "What makes you think I'd have money?"

"You might have saved some from the housekeeping money," I said. "A little here and there. It adds up."

Kate said, "Peyton has plenty of money, but he never gave me any. Oh, he'd buy me anything I wanted. All I had to do was ask, not even ask sometimes. But money —no. He knew I'd run away if he gave me money."

I said quietly, "Is that why you stole so much?"

I got a slap in the face for that, but it was more a token than a real slap. She felt she had to do it to show how outraged she was. "You son of a bitch!" she raged pretty convincingly. "I never stole a cent from that man."

"I shouldn't have said steal."

"It doesn't matter what you call it. I didn't steal anything. I left Mexico with nothing but the clothes on my back. A buggy, a horse and my clothes. Nothing else."

"Not even a few pieces of jewelry?"

She knew that I knew a woman would take jewelry before anything else. Maybe even before cash. "Well, yes, I did take a few pieces, but they belonged to me," she admitted, pausing to see how I took it. Then she went on. "They won't bring much. Jewelers have you at their mercy when you go to them to sell jewels. What I've told you is the truth, Saddler."

It was hard to think of this woman being at anyone's mercy. The role didn't fit her, like a 50-year-old actress playing a schoolgirl. "A little bird told me you got more than a few jewels, darlin'. Money and gold. Mexican Doubles, a whole lot of them, this little bird said."

"Go fuck yourself," Kate said. "You and your little bird! You've been listening to dirty rumors like the rest of them. My God! if I had money and gold, would I be here?"

"You might," I said. "Here you have some protection. On the move, Ballard would have detective agencies after you. They'd find you—a good chance of it—and then he'd find you. I think that's why you're staying on in Dragoon Wells."

"I don't like the way you're talking. It sounds as if you aren't going to help me. I thought you were better than that, Saddler."

That wasn't so bad. At least she hadn't accused me of tricking her into bed. "Look, are we friends or not?" I wanted to know. "Don't you want to share with a good friend?"

Kate rolled away from me and lay sulking. "Even if I had it, I wouldn't share it with you. One thing you're not and that's a friend. I'm not saying I have the money, but if I did, if I gave some of it to you—you'd probably run out on me."

She fought me when I tried to pull her close. In the end, she let me win. I said, "If you had money and you shared it I probably wouldn't leave you in the lurch. That's the truth, darlin'."

"Darlin', my ass!" Kate said. "What do you know about the truth?"

"As much as you. Truth's got nothing to do with it. I see it as a deal between two friends. I think I should get something out of it."

Kate reached for my crotch. It had only been a few minutes since our wrestling match, but I was ready to go again. "Isn't what you got enough?" she asked.

"I wouldn't give a damn if you didn't have money," I said. "But you do and I'd like a few dollars."

Kate laughed and stroked harder. "I can manage that much."

"More than a few," I said.

"How much more?"

"What would you say to half?"

"I'd say shit."

"So we haven't made any progress?" I said.

Instead of answering, Kate climbed on top of me, and for a while money was forgotten. But when it was over for the second round, we got back to it again.

"You could call *that* progress," Kate said, lying back with her eyes closed.

I felt like I'd been over the jumps and back again. "Why be such a hog about it?" I said, tired but happy. "It's not like you'll be left short. Half of fifty thousand is still a lot."

Kate opened her eyes and regarded me with deep suspicion. "How did you get that figure?"

"From Danziger."

"He's a liar and so are you."

"It's still a good deal," I said.

"What about a quarter share?" Kate said quickly, feeling she had worn me down. She had.

"A quarter share of fifty thousand?"

"A quarter share of twenty thousand. I have twenty, not fifty. That's five thousand."

"I know how much it is. I liked fifty thousand better. A quarter share of that is . . . ."

Kate said, "Take it or go fuck yourself. How much I have is none of your fucking business, Saddler. If I say I have twenty, then twenty it is. My friend, I put up with a lot to get what I have. If five thousand isn't enough for you, you greedy shit, then you can just pull your prick. What's it going to be?"

"Sold to the lady with the red hair," I said, reaching for her again. "I'll just have to trust you."

"Look who's talking," Kate scoffed. "You think I was lying about how hard it was to get what I have. My friend, after I had that fight with my father, I had to leave here with nothing. He thought I was still lying down for the marshal. I wasn't—we had a fight too—but my father thought I was. I told him to mind his own fucking business. I was free, white, if not twenty-one. After that I traveled all over, waitressing, clerking in stores. I was looking for a rich man, but the ones I found seemed to know what I was after. They'd buy me things, but no wedding ring. I got to know an awful lot about men, Saddler. Too much. When I met Peyton I was dancing in a saloon in Brownsville, Texas. Peyton isn't wanted in Texas so he could go there. I don't know how old Peyton is, over fifty anyway, but when he asked me to marry him I jumped at the chance."

"But you got to know him better," I said, ready to ward off a slap.

It didn't come. "That's what happened. Peyton isn't much good to any woman anymore. Maybe he never was. He was no good for me. He'd get in bed with me, usually

76

drunk, and we'd try it again. Nothing. Then he'd get mad as if I was the cause. When he started to beat me I knew I had to get out. So I waited till one night when he got stinking drunk after another failure in the bedroom. Drunk, then cursing, then sleeping. I bribed one of his Mexicans to get me to the border. And here I am, sonny boy. If you double-cross me, I'll cut your balls off. Not that I want to castrate you, you rat. That's my story, shitkicker. I always shake hands when I make a deal."

We shook hands solemnly and she pressed herself close to me. "I only talk tough when I'm scared, Saddler. Right now, I'm scared to death. Promise you won't let Peyton get me."

I hoped I'd be alive to keep my word.

EIGHT

Bed didn't have much interest after Kate got out of it,
but it was still dark and too early to get up. The sweet
smell of Kate was on me and on the bedclothes. Our
exertions had made a tangle of the bed, and it seemed a
shame to straighten it, to put it back the same cold way it
was before she came. I was getting fond of that bed and
would always have fond memories of the two lovely
ladies I'd tussled with in it. By itself, that made up for the
trouble I was in.

I was in it, sure enough. I didn't think Danziger would
try to get me in the jail if he hadn't tried it outside. Doing
things the underhand way was more his style. A fixer and
a crook wouldn't go against the law head-on unless there
was some other way. I knew I'd been wrong in not killing
him and I was taking my chances after that. But it was
just as well that I hadn't. I couldn't kill him and stay on.
Besides, it would be the finish of Johnny Callahan.
Danziger's political cronies would see that the governor
yanked him out of there, maybe put him on trial for

conspiracy to commit murder. Then, too, I wouldn't be of any use to Kate, if I had to run. Ballard would send his gunmen, and that would be the end of it.

There was gray light in the window, but the town was still quiet. Thinking of Kate, I didn't blame Ballard for wanting her back. Any man with balls would want her back. I figured that Danziger wasn't too happy with the job he'd been given. There must have been a lot of money and a lot of threats to make him do what he was doing. All his life, Danziger had weaseled his way out of tight corners, always counting on his brain to survive. By the looks of him, it had worked pretty well in the past. Danziger wasn't the kind of man to believe in killing. It wasn't good business; besides, he probably didn't like it, like most sane men. Now, for the first time, he was mixed up in a dangerous game he couldn't quit. There were no strings he could pull to get him out of this one. Ten to one, Ballard had enough on Danziger to jail him for life. That and the money was why he was in Dragoon Wells. He would order killing if nothing else worked. But first he'd work with the money. I was sure of that.

The sun was warming the street when I unbarred the jail door and took a look at the town. Sun was full in the street by the time I dipped my head in a bucket of cold water and smoked one of Johnny's cigars. I didn't want to come back to any surprises; so I locked the jail and took the key with me when I went to eat at the old man's.

"Better have the steak and eggs instead of ham and eggs," he told me. I kind of liked the old gent, about the only man in town who wasn't looking daggers at me. "Don't want to try the ham on you. Don't look cured right. Not poisonous, just not cured right. I'll throw it in the pea soup. That ought to fix it."

Eggs, cracked into fat, began to sizzle. The old man made good coffee and the first hot cup burned away some of my gloomy mood. "Know any men I could hire as deputies?" I asked him.

The old man turned the eggs and came back with the

coffee pot. He was pretty bright for an old man who had spent his life frying eggs. "I'd have to say no, Mr. Saddler. A few days ago I would have said sure. Times are bad hereabouts, money scarce. A few days ago you'd be knee-deep in deputies. Not now, I'm afraid. Talk's been going round since that gunman got himself killed by the Flannerys. People know it's about that Flannery girl who won't go back to her husband. They's saying that's what she ought to do."

"Would you send her back?"

The old man said, "I'd have to say no to that. Of course, at my age there ain't much to be scared of. What can Ballard do to me, break my china? Kill me? I'm fixing to put a bullet in my head when I get too old to work. What do you think, Mr. Saddler?"

I got up and left him money. "I think you might send Danziger some of that ham. If you see a man looks like a deputy—grab him."

"Not a chance," the old man said.

On this morning at least, Danziger wasn't an early riser. Rice still hadn't come back to town. When he returned it wouldn't be escorting a new schoolteacher. My guess was that he had headed for the nearest telegraph office. That would be at the railroad, about two long days' ride from town. Danziger was sending for reinforcements. It couldn't be anything else.

I went back to the jail, and for want of something to do, I cleaned my guns. I was in the middle of it when I heard loud voices in the street. When I looked out it wasn't a lot of people. It was just Danziger flapping his mouth. All spruced up in a fresh suit, he was handing a line of bullshit to the banker, who was also the mayor. It wasn't a job that paid money, but McLandress liked it, liked the title. In the street it was hot and quiet and I could hear Danziger's every word. Most likely he wanted me to hear.

Danziger looked my way when I came out the jail door. Then he put his arm around McLandress's shoulder and said again that Dragoon Wells most definitely was a town with possibilities. McLandress, that sour, puffy man, wanted to believe what he was being told.

"I'm heartened you say that, Mr. Danziger," he said.

Danziger shoved on more horseshit, but even for him, flannel-mouth that he was, it wasn't easy to list all the wonders of Dragoon Wells. He did his best, and he was damn good at it. He stayed away from the cattle business because that wasn't too bad, and for smart ranchers like the Flannerys it was better than that.

Danziger turned his benign gaze on the dusty town. "I see this little city coming back to life," he declared. "Let me put it this way. My associates are definitely interested in what this town has to offer. You may depend on that, sir."

McLandress, already seeing a flow of money into his bank, liked everything Danziger was hinting at. But he was impatient to hear what it was.

"Pardon my reticence, sir," Danziger said. "But there are business reasons, if you get my meaning. At the moment it's confidential. If I disclosed my information before the time is ripe, other towns would be clamoring for attention. We can't let that happen, can we?"

Ever the man of business, McLandress said, "Absolutely not, sir. I understand perfectly. Perhaps a little talk later in my office. At your convenience, of course."

Taking the cigar out of his mouth, Danziger said with a wink, "It's a pleasure to do business with a man who knows business."

Danziger pretended to see me for the first time. "Good morning to you, Deputy."

He was in high good humor, and I guess he thought he had found a way to get around me. McLandress just gave me a stiff nod. Ah, I thought, if you only knew that I've been fucking your lovely daughter.

"What're you promising to do?" I asked Danziger. "Move the capital down this way?"

McLandress glowered at me. "We were having a

81

private business talk, nothing to do with you. I'd be obliged if you kept out of it."

Danziger grinned. He liked having me there. Lattigo was watching from the porch of the hotel. Danziger laughed at my little joke. "Afraid I don't have that much pull, Deputy. Tell you the truth, this snug little town would suit me fine. A country boy born and bred is what I am. Give me the quiet life, sir, good, hard-working people for neighbors. I ask you, what more could a man want?"

"You said it," I said.

McLandress wanted me gone. "I said this was a private talk. It concerns the very lifeblood of this community. Private, I said."

"Not the way Danziger yells, Mr. McLandress."

The banker bristled. "*Mister* Danziger," he said, climbing up on his high horse. "You have no better manners than Marshal Callahan."

Old Earl, friend of the common man, stuck up for me. "No need to call down the Deputy, Mr. Mayor. Like the man said, 'Call me by any name you like, just don't call me late for supper.'"

"Why don't you ask Danziger about the Flannerys?" I said to McLandress. "You know who they are?"

This time McLandress looked uncomfortable. "I'm not about to ask Mr. Danziger anything. He is known to me by reputation, which is more than I can say for you."

"Mr. Danziger is loved by one and all," I said.

Nothing I said bothered the man from Tucson. "If I didn't know you better, I'd think you didn't like me."

"Ask him about the Flannery girl," I said to McLandress.

"Absolutely not." McLandress was sweating in the hot sun. He turned away from me. "You feel like having that talk now, Mr. Danziger? Where we won't be interrupted."

"I wish you wouldn't stay mad at the Deputy," Danziger said, poking the banker in the ribs in his backroom way. "A good lawman is a little suspicious of everybody, even of a man like me that's known all over. About the talk, we'll have that later if you don't mind. I hope you got some good whiskey. To celebrate, I mean."

I don't think McLandress ever tasted whiskey in his life, but he managed a good-fellow smile. "It'll be there, sir. It's an honor to have you in our town, and I think I speak for the rest of its citizens. I'll bid you good morning."

Danziger smiled at the banker's back and then at me. Sweat trickled from his crinkly hair and ran into his eyes. He wiped it away and stuffed his handkerchief into his sleeve.

"How did I do?" he asked in a low voice.

"Pretty good," I said. "McLandress bit hard but you didn't pull too hard on the line, you shit-faced son of a bitch."

"It's too late to kill me," Danziger said. "You missed your chance up there in the hotel."

"It can still get done."

"I think it's too late. Soon it'll be later than that."

"Don't count on it, Danziger."

"But I do," Danziger said. "I count on money and then more money. Money solves all problems, cures all ills. It's what oils the wheels, makes the world go round. It's a powerful shame to waste it on just one woman. That's not for me to decide. I can call for more money than you'll ever see in your life. Why don't you start thinking the same way? Get yourself a wet tit and start sucking before the rush starts. Man, don't you see? No man can stand against the power of the dollar."

He wasn't saying anything I hadn't heard before. He was right about some of it, and we both knew it. But he didn't know me. I can be a mule. "You're wrong this time," I said.

"Don't be too sure," Danziger said calmly. "The only time I was wrong was when I ran for Governor of Texas. I didn't spread enough money around. I hedged when I should have gone for broke. That was a fool thing to do—I could have made it back, and more, in no time."

"You're still wrong," I said. "I'm going to prove it to you."

Danziger wiped his face again. "I guess there's no good talking to you. Nothing personal, you understand, but I'm going to turn this town against you. First with promises, then with money. The money is how I hope to do it. Usually it's the start and the finish. And if you still doubt me, I'll tell you something else. I have to get that woman back to Ballard, and there's no ifs about it."

"You'd better start running," I said. "You're not going to get her."

"Run! You trying to be funny, Deputy." Danziger didn't laugh, didn't smile. "Where could I run that Ballard wouldn't find me?"

That night Danziger gave a party at the hotel. I didn't get an invitation, but that must have been an oversight. Anyway, I don't think lawmen get invited to parties. People figure they'll just show up. They don't get invited but nobody keeps them out when they come to drink the free liquor.

Killing Danziger and Lattigo still was a good idea, but it came to me that a better way would be for Kate Flannery to get the hell out of Dragoon Wells. No woman, no war. The more I thought about it, the better I liked it.

I sat on the porch watching things being carried into the hotel. A man from Casey's delivered a whole wagonload of whiskey and beer. There was even going to be food. I thought about Kate and didn't like the thought of having her gone. Yet I was willing to make the sacrifice. There were places she could go where Ballard wouldn't be likely to find her. Danziger thought Ballard was the Devil himself. I didn't credit him with that much power. I'd be losing money on the deal, but that would be better than all the bloodshed I saw ahead if she stayed. In the beginning, I thought there was a chance of making Danziger back down. Now I knew I'd be wrong. He couldn't. He was getting old and he wouldn't know how to run. I knew he would stay even if it got him killed. It probably would. Me too.

With Kate gone, all I'd have to do was wait around until Johnny got well. I owed him something. He hadn't given me the job to start a war. After he came back on his own two feet, I would head for the border. Kate was heavy on my mind, and it would take time to forget her. I'd manage to do that. So far though, my idea was all one sided. Kate wasn't a Flannery for nothing; there was a fair chance that she would tell me to go fuck myself. I grinned. I'd much rather fuck her.

I was still thinking about her when the band struck up over at the hotel. All the windows were open and the music blared out into the street. People passed the jail on the way to the party. A few nodded. It was getting dark and lights came on and people straggled to the hotel from all directions, stiff in their Sunday clothes. And it wasn't just a party for the town: people came in farm wagons and on horseback. I listened to the music for a while.

I had no idea how to get Kate out of Dragoon Wells. Sure as hell, her folks couldn't be talked to in any reasonable way. This time I'd get shot. I could rope her and tie her, but where would I take her? I gave up that idea, though I must say I liked it. I went inside and drank some of Johnny's bourbon and was ready for the party.

I corked the bottle and went to the door. The band sounded like a mechanical piano assisted by a fiddle, a banjo, a horn. It was pretty terrible. I gave it a while. No party ever gets going good until the first few bottles have been emptied. I walked down to the livery stable to have a look at my horse. Calvin worked there when he wasn't at the jail. He was sitting on a barrel trying to read a book by lantern light. The name of the book was *Great Captains of Industry;* Calvin moved his lips as he read.

Calvin slept in one of the empty stalls and his straw-filled mattress had been unrolled for the night. A plate of beans lay in front of him on another barrel, and now and then he reached out without looking and forked beans into his mouth. When I came in he put his finger in the book to mark his place.

"Who'd you say was the smartest—Diamond Jim Brady or Bet-A-Million Gates?" he wanted to know. To him it was a serious question.

"I think Gates has more money so that makes him the smart one," I said. "Besides, he doesn't wager as much as he lets on. Any strange horses come in today?"

"Nary a one," Calvin answered. "I'd of told you if there was. Just the regulars and yours."

Calvin told me he was planning to be a millionaire when he got old enough to do it. I said that was a dandy idea, so keep on studying the books. Calvin, eager to get back to his book, said he would. He was back in the dream world of millionaires by the time I left the stable.

In the days when Dragoon Wells had dreams of its own, the man who owned the hotel put in a ballroom. It wasn't any bigger than a country church; still, it was a ballroom. Now they had swept it out and opened the doors to let some air in. It opened off the lobby and the noisemakers were banging away when I got there. The clerk's face got as grim as the music when I walked in. I winked at him and joined the festivities.

People were dancing like people who hadn't paid for their liquor. Two of Casey's boys were behind a make-shift bar, planks laid across iron trestles, pouring as fast as they could grab the bottles. There were two punchbowls for the ladies, one with booze, one without. Men not wanting to wait for the bartenders were helping themselves to the whiskey. There was plenty of it, none of it Gilligan's Breathless.

Looking benevolent, Mayor McLandress was ladling punch for the ladies. I looked for Laurie but didn't see her, and there wasn't a Flannery in the room. Danziger was doing his damnedest to charm the bloomers off Mrs. McLandress. Lattigo was there too, never wandering far from his boss. The band cut loose again and Danziger led Mrs. McLandress out on to the floor.

McLandress spilled punch when he saw me. I gave him a wink and went to the bar for a drink. Out on the floor Danziger and the banker's lady were creaking around. I drank the whiskey, a fair bourbon, and poured another.

Danziger was manfully enduring the dance, a waltz, but he got out just in time before the band launched into what they thought was a polka. The men who owned the lumber company and buried dead gunmen came in with their wives. Danziger bowed to the undertaker's lady and whacked the undertaker on the back. The lumber man's fat wife giggled and said Mr. Danziger was a naughty man.

Danziger chucked her under the chin and turned to look at me, knowing I was an interested spectator. Not wanting to lose Danziger's attention, the fat woman clutched at his arm. It wasn't every day that a gallant like Earl Danziger blundered into her life. Still looking at me, Danziger squeezed her high on the arm. She giggled again and her husband broke out in a wintry smile.

"You're terrible, Mr. Danziger," the fat woman said.

Danziger told her to go and dance with her "beau." The fat lady didn't like that though she nearly laughed her fat head off. As the husband led her away, Danziger called out, "Till we meet again." The fat woman laughed and bullied her husband all over the floor.

"You're drinking—good!" Danziger said to me. "What do you think of my little get-together." He took my glass and went to get it filled, then came back with my drink and one for himself.

"I think it's a fine party," he said.

"You forgot to invite Mrs. Ballard," I said.

Danziger didn't answer until he stuck his face in his drink. "Wrong, my friend. I did invite her. I invited all the Flannerys. I thought we could talk this out over a few drinks. Could be they'll show up later."

"You won't like it if they do."

Down at the end of the still dusty ballroom, the mechanical piano gave out a grinding sound as if it needed oil. The musicians played louder to cover it. They were game gents, those musicians, and while they worked their asses off for the dancers, one of Casey's boys brought pitchers of cold beer to the bandstand.

Danziger smiled at me, thinking he had it all wrapped up. "You'll be pleased to hear I decided not to move the capital from up north. Too much trouble. What I'm going to do is reopen the mines in this town."

"That'll take some doing," I said. "The mines are all played out. You saw the tip heaps when you rode in. That's all that's left."

"It can be done," Danziger said.

"They won't believe you," I said. "What was in the mines has been taken out. McLandress knows that, they all do. You can't mine what isn't there."

"Wrong again," Danziger said. "Those tip heaps, as you call them, are still full of valuable ore. In the old days they didn't know how to get everything out. Now they do. That's a fact, Deputy. Ask any mining engineer. They're starting to do it all over. It's going to mean new prosperity for this town."

"If it gets done."

"Well, yes, that's a consideration. They scratch my back and I'll scratch theirs. That's how it works."

Back at the punchbowl, McLandress was trying to listen; so Danziger raised his voice to a vote-getting level. "This town is going back on the map, Mr. Saddler. There'll be a new era of prosperity. You have my personal guarantee on that. Dragoon Wells is going to be one lively town."

"Livelier than you think," I said. "I don't give a shit what you do—you're not getting that girl."

The piano was beginning to sound like a keg of nails being rolled down a hill, and after trying to fix it, the hotel man pulled the lever that shut it off. McLandress jumped into the sudden silence and called on Danziger to make a speech. Acknowledging the applause, Danziger said he'd be glad to make a speech—"A short one, folks"—provided they didn't close down the bar. That got even more applause and Danziger went one way and I went another. Going out I snagged a full quart from the bar and went back to the jail.

NINE

Laurie was waiting for me in the shadows, and I put my gun away as she came out. She was wearing a caped coat with a hood over a flowered nightdress. Red sateen slippers peeped out from under the hem of the coat.

"I know," I said. "Your father will kill you if he finds you here. Why aren't you at the party?"

She was in a hurry to get inside the jail. "My father wouldn't let me go. He thinks I looked flushed. If he only knew what I'm flushed about. Maybe it's more than the flush. He said you were sure to be there, and he doesn't think I should be seen talking to a man like you."

I smiled at her. "Your father's right. Besides, I don't feel much like talking."

Laurie giggled. "Me neither. What have you been thinking about us? Have you decided? If I don't get out of this town I'm going to go crazy. What's taking you so long to make up your mind? Wasn't it good with me?"

I didn't know what to say. Most men would have grabbed her, grabbed the money, and been out of town inside of an hour. Nobody had to get shot—the money belonged to her, sort of. I liked this crazy girl, and it galled me to act like a shitkicker. Without the money she would have been dandy; with it she was a lonesome cowboy's dream.

Laurie came up close to me and I kissed her. "I'm going to be so good to you that you'll have to go with me," she said. "I'm going to break your back. That's a terrible thing to say, isn't it?"

"Sounds like poetry to me," I said, and we went in to bed like an old married couple. But nothing we did in there was old or married. I hadn't changed the bedclothes since Kate, and Laurie sniffed suspiciously.

"You been putting something on your hair?" she asked, but her voice trailed off when I began to take off her clothes. The people at the party weren't having half the good time we were. She was right about the second time being better. A man and a woman get to know each other's bodies after the first time. She bucked under me as I put it into her, and she kept on bucking. God! She was a lovely thing, soft yet firm, strong but yielding, and I drove it in and out of her until her eyes were wild and when her climax came she shuddered her way through it, and then she had another and another. . . .

"We'll have years of this ahead of us," she whispered. I knew this wasn't true. Months maybe, but not years. No chance of that, even if I wanted to drag it out that long. But I said nothing. Laurie went on with, "Years of teaching each other, trying it in new ways, doing it in different ways. I have a French book my father doesn't know about. He'd have a fit of apoplexy if he knew I did. It has drawings. In one picture they're doing it dog-style. The woman gets down on her hands and knees and the man mounts her in that position. Does that sound good?"

"Sounds wonderful," I agreed.

"Want to try it?"

"Not right now. A cold, bare jail and a narrow bed

isn't the place for that."

"That's true. It would be better in a comfortable hotel room with thick, soft carpets and absolute privacy. Then we'll try it that way and all the other ways too."

"I'm looking forward to it," I said, which was no more than true.

"But we'll have to get there first," she prompted me, getting back to the subject of looting her father's bank. Her foxy little mind never strayed far from that. "We'll be off the same night we get the money. The money is mine by right. Anyway, what's my father going to do? Call in the Arizona Rangers to hunt down his own daughter? He won't do anything because there would be too much scandal. It could harm him in the banking community. If he can't control his own daughter, et cetera. And think of the fun the newspapers would have with him. My father is not a popular man—too tight with loans, too many foreclosures. We have nothing to fear, Saddler. A bank robbery without risk. I know you're going to say yes."

"I probably am," I said, thinking I'd be a fool if I didn't. But we didn't have to rush off that very minute. There was some unfinished business to be seen to. Business that was really none of my business. Still and all. . . .

At the moment my unfinished business was with Laurie. This time I lay on my back with my shaft pointing straight up. Laurie sat on it so it penetrated deep, and she gasped at the way it went in. I didn't have to do a thing. She moved her ass up and down. Her knees were on both sides of me, and she used them for leverage, raising and lowering her ass that way. She was young and supple and lightly built, so she was able to move without effort. Every time her ass moved down it seemed as if my shaft was sticking right up into her middle. It drove me wild. I squeezed her breasts at the same time, and she moaned as much from that as from her up-and-down movement on my cock.

"This position is from that French picture book," she whispered, hardly able to get the words out. Her face was strained but happy and full of healthy lust.

Hurrah for French picture books, I thought.

Now her ass was moving faster and faster as she worked up to her come. Then her ass came down hard and stayed there while she shuddered all over. She tried a few more up-and-down movements, but she was too weakened from orgasms to be able to manage more than a few. That was enough for me and I shot straight up into her. She came again and shook so hard I was afraid she was going to faint. But she didn't and after a while the trembling stopped and she smiled at me. Then she stretched out beside me in Johnny Callahan's bed and whispered, "It was so good I thought I was going to die."

"It wouldn't be a bad way to go. There's nobody like you, Laurie. I'm not just saying that."

"I hope not, Saddler. I feel as if I can do anything with you. And I want you to do anything with me or to me. I feel no shame with you."

"Why should you? You're a woman and I'm a man. We both like the same thing and there's no holding back."

She sounded serious when she said, "That's right. There's no pretending, no taking advantage. I don't know how honest you are about some things; but you're honest with me. Not once have you been rough with me."

"Why would I be rough?"

"Some men like to do it in a rough way. I know. I was with a man in Charleston—I was sixteen—and he used me like an animal. From behind, if you know what I'm saying. He just turned me on my face and rammed it in there. It hurt and if I cried he beat me when he finished. I shouldn't have gone with him, but I needed a man; and I knew him and I thought I could trust him."

"Stay away from rough men, men like that," I said.

"Oh I will, Saddler. From now on I'll stay with you."

"Good idea."

93

"They call that buggery, don't they?"

"They do, but you don't have to go on with this. You've told me and that's the end of it."

But she wasn't ready to let it go. You might say little Laurie had sex, in all its variations, on her feverish little mind.

"Have you ever been buggered, Saddler?"

"No," I said firmly. "I have not."

"It will be so nice in Mexico City," she said, abruptly changing the subject. I was glad of the change. Discussing buggery is not like discussing the weather. Give me the weather or the price of pork.

"Would you like a drink?" I asked her, and when she said yes I gave her a drink of Daniel's.

"Ah," she said, "not as good as sex, but good."

We lay quietly listening to the thump of the music coming from the hotel. "Don't take too long, Saddler, please don't," she whispered. "I know I said that before, but I feel the wildness building up in me and I have to let it go. If it can't be you, then I'll have to find someone else. I have to get the money before my father makes me marry some old geezer. Or some young geezer. He keeps talking about it. Then all my chances will be gone."

Right then I heard them coming. The music stopped and they were on their way. Laurie heard them too, men with loud voices. "Oh God! I have to go out the back way. Kiss me, Saddler, and please say yes."

The voices stopped before they reached the jail. I looked around to see if Laurie had left anything. She hadn't. Then McLandress yelled from outside, "You in there, Deputy?"

I yelled for them to come in. Whatever it was, Danziger was sure to be behind it. McLandress didn't come in first. Instead, a giant of a man I'd seen at the party opened the door. I had seen him glowering at me in the hotel, but put it down to nothing special. Now I knew it had to be more than that. He'd been drinking or dancing or both; sweat rolled off him like rain, and there were widening stains under the armpits of his heavy dark suit. His blond hair had been clipped so short in the Prussian style that his pink scalp showed through.

"Where's the Mayor?" I asked him.

The banker bulled his way through the crowd and came in followed by as many as could get in. I'd seen them before, the lumber company man and some others. None of them looked like working men; money-hungry smalltown businessmen is what they were. They shuffled in silently, and I knew McLandress was going to do the talking. Danziger had pulled the strings and here they were!

"You had more room back at the hotel," I said to the banker. I think I sounded friendly enough. I didn't have a thing against the stupid bastards. Money smells as sweet in my nose as it does in any man's, but I won't grub for it. That's what they were doing, sucking up to a schemer like Danziger.

It pained McLandress to be polite to me. The banker, being a banker, was the kind to make a sour face at a poor man's hello, then run to lick a rich man's boots.

McLandress cleared his throat noisily. "We've come to talk to you," he began. "It's time we had a talk."

I did my best to look agreeable. "What do you want to talk about?"

They mumbled back, some not liking me, some maybe even hating me because I was an obstacle that had to be moved and they weren't sure how to do it. I was standing between them and the money, and that's enough to make any businessman hate you. They believed all they had to do was to get rid of me and the money would come rolling in. Looking at the mealymouth bunch of shits, I was almost ready to concede that Danziger had more class. He was what he was and didn't pretend to be anything else.

Only the big man with the clipped head wasn't afraid of me, and I wondered again who he was. I knew McLandress was trying to work up enough nerve to tell me to quit, I was fired, or whatever. Before he spoke, the banker looked to make sure the big blond brute was still there. Then I got it. This was the man they wanted to put in as town marshal. After I decided that, I began to watch him more carefully. Rough stuff, if it came, would come from him.

"This has to be said, Mr. Saddler," the banker began, puckering his womanish lips. Behind him there was a murmur of agreement. I crossed my legs to make myself more comfortable, and wouldn't you know it, the rifle I held ended up pointing straight at the banker's jowly face.

At first, McLandress was like a rabbit looking at a snake. "Let me save time and say it for you," I said. "You want me to leave, but I don't want to leave. And maybe you want to know why I've been talking so tough to Danziger. Because he's a sneaking nightcrawler, is the answer. Danziger works for a man that burned a whole town and murdered its people. You want to hear more?"

"There's no proof of what you're saying," McLandress protested. "Anyway, the war's been over a long time."

"How long is long?" I asked them. I was talking to McLandress, but the question was for everyone. "There's no limit on what he did. That's the man you're pimping for, catching runaway women for. Slave catchers and pimps, that's what you are, all of you."

"We didn't come here to be insulted," McLandress blustered. "Least of all by the likes of you. You want to know how much we care about this Flannery woman? Not a thing—there's your answer. She was never one of us when she lived here. If sending her back means life to this town, then to blazes with her. To blazes with the rest of the Flannerys. They're no neighbors of ours. Mr. Danziger is about to give this town a chance and we're going to take it. I'll make it short—we want you to get out."

"Can't be done," I said, keeping an eye on the big man.

"You won't listen," the big man said.

96

"Then don't stand in the way," McLandress said. "Let things take their course. Nobody's asking you to hand over the girl. Keep out of it, that's all you have to do. That's what Callahan would do. I wish to God he was here instead of you."

"But he's not," I said. "Anyway, I don't know that he wouldn't do the same. That's not the question. I'm the marshal. You think I should let those bastards have the girl, go fishing or get drunk while they're taking her back to that butcher. No, sir."

McLandress sucked in so much air his lardy face turned red. He cleared his throat, getting ready to fire his big gun at me. The big gun was a weary-faced old man with Horace Greeley whiskers and a beaver hat. He trembled like a leaf—a drinker.

"If you please, Judge," the banker said, pulling him forward by a very frail arm. The old man jumped when his name was called and he dropped a heavy law book. When he got under the light I saw how old and poor he was, and how scared. McLandress grabbed the book off the floor and thrust it at him so hard he nearly knocked him down.

"Go easy with him," I said.

It was plain that the Judge hadn't heard a kind word for a very long time. Every miserable town in the West has a judge like this one.

"Thank you, Marshal Saddler, my name is Isaac Ferguson." He nodded at me and found it hard to stop once he had started.

The banker was puffed up like a rooster about to make a surprise attack on a hen. It's a wonder he didn't crow, and now that his jowls were red he looked very much like a rooster. I hoped he wasn't going to be too disappointed.

The Judge couldn't find his page and the banker had to help him. The book was the laws of the Arizona Territory and I knew what was coming. It didn't mean diddly-shit to me. The Judge found it easier to see after he finally discovered his spectacles in his pants pocket. They were dirty and one of the lenses was cracked down the middle.

Blinking at me, holding the law book in shaky hands, he told me I wasn't any kind of lawful lawman.

"Goddamn right," the big man said.

The Judge tried to bring the big man into focus. "Please don't interrupt, Mr. Dorfman," he said as sternly as his condition would allow. "I was about to cite the statute pertaining to the appointment of deputies and police officers of any kind."

The old man got started again and he read such and such, paragraph this and that. It boiled down that Johnny was required to send a letter to the Territorial Governor the day he appointed me. This had not been done, the Judge declared. Therefore, I had never been a legal deputy marshal.

"That's the law, Mr. Saddler. You notice that I address you as Mister instead of Deputy or Marshal. You have been holding office contrary to the laws of this territory. As an officer of the court—that's what a lawyer is—I direct you to surrender your badge and to vacate these premises. Forthwith, sir."

I grinned at the Judge. He was a drunk but I liked him. He reminded me of a drunken uncle who died by drinking from the wrong bottle. "You read that real good, Judge," I said.

The Judge was pleased, but the banker snapped, "Read it yourself if you want to. The law is clear. It should be, even to you. What are you smiling at? This is no joking matter. If you refuse to leave this office, if you defy the law, you can be arrested and prosecuted for—for what, Judge?"

The Judge had the charge on the tip of his tongue, but it must have slipped off. "For a lot of things," he quavered.

"Correct!" McLandress said. "That's what could happen to you. However"—the banker tried to sound reasonable, almost friendly—"there's no need for that. You had no way of knowing that you were breaking the law. So we are prepared to be generous, Mr. Saddler. You've only been her a few days, but we're ready to pay you for the entire month. I think that's fair, don't you?"

"I think it's more than fair," I said. "Four thousand for four weeks is good pay in any army.".

McLandress gulped, and his stinginess warred with the greed for Danziger's money. The figure I quoted was four times what Callahan got. "Come! Come! Mr. Saddler," he blustered. "We all know that Marshal Callahan agreed to pay you five hundred. Remember, you don't have to do a thing to get it . . . plus a little bonus for your inconvenience. What do you say to seven hundred and fifty dollars?"

I told them to go fuck themselves.

It got very quiet in the jail, and I moved the rifle away from McLandress until it was pointing at Dorfman, the man they wanted to put in as the new deputy. The Judge wasn't afraid of the rifle—maybe he couldn't see it—and neither was Dorfman. All the others wanted to run, and they crowded together like panicky sheep trying to get through the same small gap.

I expected to get fists from Dorfman—not talk. The Judge had read from his book, said his piece, and it hadn't worked. Dorfman moved out in front of the others. I told him to move back—the party was over. "Danziger's shindig is still going on," I said. "Go back and suck up some more."

Only a brave man or a stupid man would crowd a man pointing a rifle at his belly. The big man was both. There was a problem about how to handle him. I had to stop him if he kept coming. I could kill him with a touch of the trigger, but what would that get me other than blood on the floor?

Dorfman, the dumb bastard, told me that I had no right to stand in the way of the town's good fortune, and I guess the lumbering fool really believed that better times were just around the corner. "You ain't got no right to mess things up for us. People are out of work. Mr.

McLandress told you what we think, what we've decided. What do you care what happens to that woman? Let her go home where she belongs. What kind of a woman is she, running off on her lawful husband?"

I stood up holding the rifle. "Get out now," I said. "Just get out. There's your answer." I snapped the lever of the rifle, putting a bullet in the chamber. They turned and ran, and it was a good thing there were no women and kids in that crowd—they'd have been trampled. Only Dorfman stayed where he was.

"You too, squarehead," I said. "Don't get stupid. You'll have to wait for the next time Callahan breaks a leg."

"You're nothing but a smartmouth," Dorfman growled. "You wouldn't talk so tough if you didn't hold that gun."

"That's why I'm holding it. Get out quick."

Dorfman shook his thick head. "You're the one that's getting out, Saddler. You're through in this town."

I was tired of talking, and I didn't want to hear any more about people out of work. He was close enough to hit, so I hit him. The barrel dug in hard but it didn't knock him down, though it knocked the wind out of him. I upended the weapon and tried to get him with the stock. But he was fast and he clamped both hands on the rifle and would have tossed me along with it if I hadn't let go.

My gunbelt was slung over the back of the chair and as I turned he hit me with a punch like a mule kick that landed in the back of my head. Another man would have broken his hand but he didn't even grunt. He kicked me behind the knee while I was still falling. All I could think of was that handgun. I was close to grabbing it when the big man kicked chair and gunbelt clear across the room. I went over with the chair and he waded in with kicks. I took a flying leap and tackled him around the middle. When I got him I wished I hadn't. It was like trying to bring down a tree. There was nothing to hit him with but my fists.

We rolled on the floor and I tried to knee him in the balls. That didn't work either. He was up before me, grinning like a bastard telling me what he was going to do to me. He wasn't a flannelmouth, he meant to do it. I lowered my head and butted him in the gut. It was like using my head to batter down a door. My head hurt and it hurt worse when his big paws clamped on both sides of it. I expected a knee in the face, but that wasn't what he did. What he did was try to twist my head off my shoulders. I swear the son of a bitch lifted me off the floor by the head.

I don't know how big the bastard was, big as they come. He was at least three inches bigger than me and I'm six-one. In pounds he had me by 50 or 60. He lifted me and threw me like a sack of grain, but I didn't land as loose. My back hit the wall and I sat down hard. He grabbed up my rifle and broke it to bits on the top of the desk. He whacked until the barrel was bent and the desk was split. Then he threw the rifle away and came at me balling his fists, still talking. "I'm going to kick the living shit out of you. I'm going to kick your legs out through your back."

The only thing I could see was the broken chair. There was a leg with part of a rung still stuck to it. He didn't even try to stop me from getting it. He came at me with his hands out wide, ready to grab when I swung. I swung at his face and he blocked it but took a crack on the forearm. If it hurt he didn't show it. He didn't try to take the chair leg away from me, not at first. The next time I just feinted with the chunk of wood. He moved to block it and I hit him along the side of the head. His ear puffed up as soon as the blow landed. The mad grin on his face didn't change.

I got him with another crack on the head. I swung again and he blocked the blow with his open hand. His fingers closed like a steel trap. I hung onto the chair leg and he knocked me loose with a punch delivered by the other hand. He hit me on the shoulder with the chair leg before he tossed it away. He lifted his fists, huge and knobby, so I could see what he was going to use on me.

"These are all I need, little man," he said.

I went at him again using every dirty trick I knew. I know plenty of dirty tricks and at least one should have worked. He grunted when I landed a kick to his knee. That was all he did—grunt! Too much meat and muscle covered his bones to do any harm. Coming in hard, he crowded me against the back wall, making no effort to block the punches I threw at his meaty face. Then he started body punching, which was what I was afraid he would do.

The stink of sweat and liquor gusted in my face. My shoulder hurt like hell from the blow I had taken with the chair leg. He hit me again and pulled me away from the wall. A 1000-pound grizzly wouldn't have been any harder to fight. He grabbed me by the shirt and pulled. I went sliding across the top of the desk while some of the shirt stayed in his hand, and when I fell down on the other side he ran at the desk with both hands and tried to crush me against the wall. It was coming at me when I jumped on top of the desk while it was still moving and kicked him in the face.

His hands were spread wide pushing and his head was bent and the kick got him right under the chin and knocked him halfway across the room. I dived from the top of the desk, but he caught me in midair and threw me hard. I hit the stove and knocked the plate lifter and the plate from the top of it. Flames licked up as he came at me again. I knew he was boring in for the kill.

He ran at me and I sidestepped and tripped him in the direction of the stove. He yelled for the first time when his hands grabbed at the stove, and before he could turn I jumped on his back and forced his face down into the flames. There was a quick sizzling sound as the flames burned off his eyebrows and the front of his hair. I jockeyed up on his back to get more leverage. I grabbed the back of his head and pressed it deeper into the fire. It was like riding a buffalo in its death throes. He screamed and kicked as the fire ate at his face. Then, screaming madly, he pitched me over his head.

I came down so hard I thought I'd broken my back but I hadn't and then I was up again. Dorfman heard me and ran toward the sound, but he couldn't see. His face was a mass of burned flesh and his hands fumbled at the air, as if they didn't belong to him. I dodged him easily and got my beltgun off the floor. A moment before I would have used it. Now there was no longer any need. He turned and lunged again and I hooked my toe around his ankle and brought him down with a twist and kicked him in the side of the head. I had to kick him again in the same place before he shuddered and lay still.

I figured McLandress and the town fathers hadn't gone far. They were out in the dark trying to sneak away, and it took a shot fired in the air to bring them back. "Go fetch the doctor," I yelled at them. "You pushed Dorfman into this. Get the doctor or I'll get you!"

I went back inside and closed the door. Dorfman lay on the floor like a dead bear. I bent down to look at his eyes, maybe he was blind. I hoped he wouldn't die.

The doctor came in after a while and looked at the wreckage of the office. "My God! Did you do that to Hansy Dorfman! I guess you did. I'll say this, he had it coming a long time. Many's the man I doctored that had business with that squarehead. Now it's his turn to need the black bag."

I drank whiskey while the doctor saw to Dorfman. The doctor took the bottle and poured a trickle of whiskey into Dorfman's blackened mouth. He began to groan and I asked the doctor if maybe I shouldn't put the irons on him in case he got lively again.

"Not necessary," the doctor said, drinking whiskey from the bottle before he handed it back to me. "Hansy is going to be a good boy for a while. Fetch that lamp down close, will you? I want to see if he's blind."

I held the lamp while the doctor poured medical alcohol in a wad of cotton and dabbed at Dorfman's eyes. Then he threw away the dirty cotton and poked Dorfman in the ribs. "Try to open your eyes, Hansy. It's the doctor."

Dorfman's eyes fluttered open, and the doctor told me to turn the lamp down low. That done, he struck a sulphurhead match and moved it back and forth in front of Dorfman's eyes. The eyes, rimmed by black, followed the flame.

When the light was full again, the doctor had another drink of whiskey. "He'll be able to see and he never was handsome." The doctor was a sour old man full of mean humor. "Looks like I'm going to be busy with you around, Saddler."

I took the bottle back. "Busier than you think," I said.

"Well, I don't mind that," the doctor said.

TEN

I was trying to put the desk back together when Calvin showed up to do his sweeping and told me that Dorfman wasn't going to die. It was early morning and still cool. Calvin whistled when he saw the damage and went to the stable to borrow some carpenter tools. When he came back, he said, "Mr. Bush didn't want to loan them to me, but he did when I said you'd get mad."

"Do what you can with it," I said. I was back from breakfast and not in such a good mood.

Everything was getting too complicated for an old West Texas shitkicker like me. Like it or not, I was becoming too much a part of this half-forgotten town. If I had taken one of the nine other ways to the border, it would all be happening without me. A hundred to one, I'd never heard about what happened to Callahan, or Kate, or Laurie, or any of the others. The two women had me going. I had to choose between them, and then I had to choose between the one I wanted and Callahan.

Not that I trusted either one of them. They were just using me, trying to, to get what they wanted. But that's the way of women, yeah, and men, so I didn't feel put out about it. Anyway, there's no reason why you can't like someone you don't trust. Those old boys who wrote the Constitution had a good name for it—eternal vigilance. I would have to watch them so they wouldn't try to do me dirt at the wrong time.

I had been thinking about Calvin, the only person in town, apart from the old restaurant keeper, who didn't act edgy around me. I didn't count Laurie. She was too busy thinking about herself. At least she wasn't against me.

"You think Mr. Danziger has as much money as Bet-A-Million Gates?" Calvin asked, raising dust at the same time.

"Not even as much as Diamond Jim," I said.

Calvin collected the dirt in a dustpan and dumped it into the stove. "That's what I thought. Everybody else in this town thinks he's God Almighty. Mr. Bush at the stable is talking about fixing up the place for when people start coming back to town. You think that'll ever happen?"

"Not likely," I said. "If it ever happens it won't be because of anything Danziger does. He's just leading them up the garden path." I was still thinking about Kate. "How much do you know about what's happening?"

"More than you think probably. Mr. Bush don't talk about nothing else. It's like the whole town is holding their breath waiting to see what happens with that girl. Flannery, Kate Flannery. What's so important about her, is what I'd like to know?"

Calvin was still at the age when old Bet-A-Million Gates, with his millions made from barbwire, was more interesting than any woman, even one as great looking as Kate.

I had to make it sound reasonable to the boy. "She ran away from her husband because she hates him and doesn't want to go back. The husband wants her back so bad he's willing to do anything to get her."

"She must be a good cook," Calvin said. "You're in a fix, ain't you, Mr. Saddler. I could shoot a gun if I had one. I like Mr. Callahan, but I get along better with you. You don't keep forgetting my name like he does. You want help, I'm here all the time. Don't have to get paid more than I get now."

"No guns," I said. "You think you could make it to the telegraph line in a hurry? It's a good bit from here."

"Sending for the army, huh?" Calvin put away his broom and dustpan as if he'd never need them again. "That'll shake them up, if the army comes."

I looked at Calvin, with his gangling body and lank hair. No army was going to come, I told him. "Not their business. The Governor can send the Territorial militia. But you got to send him the message."

"Me!" Calvin's eyes danced with excitement.

"I don't know anyone else," I said. "The old man that runs the restaurant might do it, but he'd take a week to get there. It has to be faster than that."

Calvin didn't like the old man for reasons of his own. "That old man would fall off and kill hisself. I'll do it for you, Mr. Saddler, and I'll do it right. What should I tell the Governor?"

I said I'd write it out for him and I did. Calvin read it aloud:

"Governor William McReynolds—gosh!—Urgently request help. Regular cavalry or mounted militia. Expect attack by renegade Peyton Ballard and Mexicans. Definite proof they are proceeding Dragoon Wells this moment. Much bloodshed if help not received immediately. Signed James Saddler. Deputy Marshal. Dragoon Wells. Arizona Territory. Acting for John P. Callahan. Marshal.

"Gosh!" Calvin said again. "You think they'll come?

107

You make it sound like an invasion, Mr. Saddler. You really got proof Ballard and the Mexicans are on their way?"

"The last part, no. It's likely they'll come. I have to go on a good guess."

"That's lying to the Governor, Mr. Saddler."

"I'm lying in a good cause."

"You'll catch hell if the Governor sends the militia and there's nobody here but Danziger and that spook that follows him about. They could put you in jail for that."

I said, "Probably they could. It'd be better than having a lot of people killed. I'll let you in on a secret—they'd have to catch me first. You sure you want to do this? People are going to be mad at you when they find out. They will. I wouldn't mix you in but I can't go myself. Say no and it's all right."

Calvin was indignant at the suggestion that he wouldn't back me in time of trouble. "This is a chance to get my name in the paper. Local boy makes daring ride to save town, like they say. Words like that. Let me explain something to you, Mr. Saddler. It's important to get your name in the paper if you want people to notice you. I read once that's why Mr. Brady wears all them diamonds and stickpins and such. People notice him and write stories about him."

Calvin paused. "The only thing, I ain't got a horse."

"Take my horse but don't get rough with him. He'll go good if you tell him. Now listen to me. Watch out for hard-looking men when you get to the telegraph. It could be that Danziger has men, a man, posted there. One of his men, Billy Rice"—I described Rice—"rode out of here and hasn't come back. Rice is the smart one, that's why Danziger sent him, I'm guessing, to telegraph for more gunmen. Look around before you send the wire to the Governor. If it doesn't look good, ride on to the next telegraph station. They can't watch all of them. They could be watching the closest one."

Calvin was awed by the extent of Danziger's villainy.

108

"You mean they'd interfere with the telegraph operator. That's a federal crime, Mr. Saddler."

"That wouldn't mean much to these men. If they kill the telegrapher, who's to say who did it? Go on now. Stoke up on some grub and take bread and meat along. You won't be stopping to eat. When we go down to the stable we'll be talking about what you're going to tell Callahan."

"That's right clever, Mr. Saddler," Calvin said, taking the money I gave him. "Maybe I should take a gun along just in case."

I said no. "Don't try too hard to get your name in the paper. I don't want you getting killed over me, over this woman. I said no gun, and don't try to sneak one."

I wasn't sure that the stable man swallowed the story about Calvin riding out to Callahan's ranch. Calvin playacted a bit too hard. He did everything but walk to the footlights and whisper to the audience, the way they do. He looked too much like the bearer of great tidings, and I think the stable man caught some of that. I knew it might be edginess on my part, but to give Calvin a good start I hung around talking to Mr. Bush, who didn't want to talk to me. That meant he wanted to run to McLandress or to Danziger himself. And he did, as soon as I was back in the jail with the door closed. The stable man hurried past, darting nervous glances at the jail. Once Danziger heard the news, it didn't mean he would send Lattigo after the boy. If he did I would follow him and kill him. I'd shoot him out of the saddle without warning and leave him where he fell. It was something Lattigo needed and I was ready to do it for him.

The stable man didn't go to the bank but right into the hotel, which meant Danziger wasn't depending only on McLandress. Danziger would be playing the old go-between's game: telling one man that he trusted him more than another. In a few minutes, the stable man came out, looking pleased with himself, and went back to his work. I waited for Lattigo but he didn't show, and an hour later, still watching, I knew he wasn't going after the boy. That gave Calvin a start, and it saved Lattigo's life. For the moment it did.

The town was still quiet, but not for long. It came to life when loud yelling started at the far end of the main street, out past the sun-rotted bandstand where no band played anymore. My first thought was that Billy Rice had come back with a bunch of gunslingers ready to take on the Flannerys. Then I decided it couldn't be that because that wasn't the direction they would come from.

I went out to see what it was and there was old Con Flannery at the head of every man and boy in his family who was capable of shooting a gun. They were up on well-brushed horses, and you should have seen how that horse hair glistened in the sun. Every man and boy carried a beltgun and a rifle, and all the rifles were well-kept Winchesters. No old iron in this lot. Con Flannery was the only rider who wasn't carrying a repeater. He had the same Creedmore Sharps, the heavy rifle it was hard to miss with if you knew anything at all about guns. By the look of him, Con Flannery knew plenty, and if a man got in the sights of that rifle, he was done for. The Creedmore was good for 1000 yards, more if a man had the eye power to see that far. It was a favorite killing weapon of the Regulators, the assassins hired by the big ranchers to do away with small ranchers and farmers. It was a beautiful and terrible gun.

Con Flannery bulked up so big on his big horse in the lead that I didn't see Kate until they were well down the street. She didn't look any too happy and wasn't wearing the range clothes she'd come in the other night. Old Con had her riding sidesaddle, no doubt deciding that to fork a horse wasn't ladylike. But she was wearing a flat-crowned gray hat and boots instead of lady shoes and lady bonnet. The hat was cinched under her chin and tilted back on her head, giving her a reckless, defiant air. It was hard for her to hide that, and she wasn't trying.

They rode on in silence, with the whole town crowding

the sidewalks to gape. Nothing like this had ever been seen on a dull morning in a dead town. It was a show of force; all they needed was a flag to make it official. I heard the window of Danziger's room going up and knew he was watching. Everybody was watching and those that came late pushed through the others to get a look. The Flannerys weren't carrying jugs of coal oil; so the town was safe for now. That's no joke. They were capable of doing it, and might yet.

They kept coming, taking no heed of the hotel. They might have been riding through a ghost town for all the notice they took of the jittery citizens. I counted 20 Flannerys and 20 rifles. Impressive, on the face of it, and I had no doubt that they would put up one hell of a fight before Ballard's pistoleros cut them down. That's what had to happen, because courage and good intentions are no match for numbers and genuine meanness. Mexicans would die but Mexicans came cheap. Ballard could field 100 border gunmen for $5,000, maybe not even that much provided they could count on light-skinned women and plunder. To get the light-complected women they would do much more than kill a bunch of Irishmen.

Con Flannery raised his hand when he came abreast of the jail. The file of riders reined in, and if they feared an ambush there was no sign of it in their faces.

"Morning, Deputy," Flannery said.

"Sure is," I said.

"Not too hot."

"Just right. Anything I can do for you, Mr. Flannery?"

Con Flannery allowed himself a sliver of smile. "Nobody does anything for me, but I'm obliged by the asking. I'm here to say a few things having to do with my only daughter Kate. I guess you haven't made her acquaintance. This is Kate, Deputy Saddler."

I hoped Flannery meant what he said about me not knowing Kate. That Creedmore makes a terrible hole. Look at it this way. If a Creedmore can knock down a grizzly, what can't it do to a man? But I couldn't read a

111

thing in the Irishman's eyes.

"Miss Flannery," I said, formal as a real china teacup.

"Deputy Saddler," she said, giving nothing away. She was a lot better at playacting than Calvin.

That ended the politeness because the next instant Flannery raised his rough voice to a full-throated roar. "Listen to me, you storekeepers and money grubbers! Listen to me good! I won't say this but the one time. There's been talk going round about my daughter. This and that, gutter talk, no need to go into it. You all know what you've been saying. There's talk about my daughter and a low, sneaking, bloody-handed son of a bitch with the name Ballard. Some of you say she ought to go back to this animal. Dirty men have come here to spread dirty money to see that she does. You think you're all going to get rich with more dirty money if she does. If this talk goes on, a lot of you are going to get killed, and that, you half-men, is a promise."

Dust stirred in the sunlight and Flannery's voice boomed on, the words coming slow but stressful. "We came here today so you can take a good look at us. I ask you to think about it. Nobody's asking your help in this—I'd rather ask help from a rat—just stay out of it. Go about your grubby little business. Putting sand in the brown sugar is a lot safer than siding against us. Honest to God, I hope you believe me—it is. And for the man who came here with the renegade's dirty money, I want him to listen too."

Con Flannery turned his h rse and looked up at the open window of Danziger's room. "Hear me, Danziger," he roared. "I know who you are and what you are. Take your shitpants gunmen and get the hell out of this town. Crawl back to Ballard and tell him what he can expect if he comes here with his Mexicans. You don't like what I'm saying, come down and face me like a man. Borrow a weapon and we'll have it out. You and me, Danziger. Nobody's going to gang up on you. You want to be a man once in your life, I'll be waiting for you at the saloon."

Flannery turned back to me and you would never believe that he had been shouting threats. "It's been said, Deputy, and they can play catch with it for a while. If they side with Ballard after this, I'll flatten this miserable place. If Ballard can threaten to burn towns, then so can I. You know what I'd do, were I you?"

"What's that, Mr. Flannery?"

"I'd find another town to marshal in. This one hasn't much of a future. If Danziger can't find the saloon I'd take it kindly if you showed him the way. Deputy, what I told the town goes for you too. Don't take this job too serious. You're not the type."

Well, I'll be fucked, I thought. There I was risking my hide to keep his beautiful daughter from being handed over to Ballard, and here he was sticking out his jaw at me. I felt like I was getting it from every side. For sure I could get awful mad at the Flannery family, if I tried. It was still a good idea to get Kate out of there. There had to be places he couldn't find her. No detective agency is that good, or there wouldn't be notorious badmen still on the loose. They never did catch Jesse James, and they were looking for him a lot harder. Which wasn't to say that Ballard wouldn't spend money looking to find her. I would too. But what the hell! I was straining my brain for nothing. I knew she wouldn't go. Call me a man who didn't know his own mind, and you'd be right. I wanted her to go, I wanted her to stay.

About the only thing I could be sure of was there wouldn't be any showdown between Flannery and Danziger, who probably knew as much about guns as he did about ethics and honesty. Not a thing.

After Con Flannery left, all the interest in town was down at Casey's saloon. Up at the jail there was nothing happening. Sitting at the wrecked desk, I wondered how long the Flannerys would stay. Unless Billy Rice turned up with a pack of gunmen there wasn't much chance of a shootout. The Flannerys wouldn't shoot up the town—not yet. They had delivered their challenge, their warning, and now it was up to McLandress to sit in the game or get out. I knew Danziger wouldn't quit what he came for, but he wouldn't push it with the Flannerys breathing fire.

The door was open and Kate came in and sat down. Close up she looked better than ever, but the thought of all those brothers and uncles and cousins put a damper on how much I wanted her. It wouldn't have done me any good if I had been ready. She was all business today. I wasn't going to get a thing but talk. Not conversation—hard talk. I was ready to do some hard talking myself. Like how was I going to get paid for my part in the deal. If the governor sent the cavalry, and if he did it fast enough, the trouble with Ballard was likely to blow over. It was one thing to take on the Flannerys, but even the pistoleros would have no stomach for the Arizona Volunteers. As spit and polish soldiers they were rotten. All they knew how to do was kill. Most of them were rabid Indian killers and Mexican haters. It would please them no end to slaughter Ballard's private army.

Even so, they weren't there, and I was. My chances of getting killed were good. So I wanted to be paid. Kate must have known that because she started in on me before I could get a chance to start in on her.

"Never mind the money; you'll get your money," she said irritably. Like most redheads she was never far from boiling over. "What kind of plans have you made, that's what I'd like to know."

I told her about sending the boy to the telegraph station, after I went to the door to check for snoopers. "Not a word about that," I said. "You tell anybody and I'll leave you flat."

"I'm not too sure you won't."

"Maybe you should take your business to another store. This one is running out of everything."

"Son of a bitch! You know you're it."

"I'm glad we got that settled. I won't let them take you. You mind if I kill Ballard? If I could do that the

Mexicans wouldn't be so feisty with the money man dead."

Kate didn't even consider it. "All the better if you can do it," she said.

"It's something to think about if nothing else works. You'd be a rich widow if he hasn't changed his will. Are you in his will?"

There was real anger now. "None of your business, Saddler. What we agreed on is all you're going to get. Not a cent more."

"I'll get it when I get it," I said. "You won't like parting with the money, but you will. You want to know something else?"

"What's that, Saddler?"

I grinned at her. "I'm glad I'm not married to you," I said.

"I wouldn't marry you if you were good looking and owned a million dollars," Kate said.

Notice how all my women keep talking about money. You'd expect that kind of gab from the homely ones. Not so. It's the beauties who like to talk about the long green. Beauties are always greedy; they have so much, they want more.

"I'd have some money if you gave me some," I said. "And don't keep telling me I'll get it later. The later you spoke about the last time is now—where is it?"

Kate got up and walked around to remind me there was more than money in this deal. She swang her hips, as we say back home, and I had to force myself to keep my mind on business. With her carrying on like that, it wasn't easy.

She spun around with a swirl of skirts. "All right, you'll get a good part of it next time I come back to town. I had it ready today, but didn't want my father asking about it."

I knew that was a lie. Unless the gold was still in the ore stage, it would have made a nice small package. But no matter, she said it was coming.

115

Kate had nothing but scorn for my avarice. That was all right. Coming from a woman as greedy as she was, it was a sort of lefthanded compliment.

"Since you won't wait, won't trust me, it can't be all money," she said, sitting down again. She straddled a chair and rested her arms on the back of it, irritable as only a redheaded beauty can be. Dear Lord! I don't know if women know what straddling a chair can do to a man. I would say they do. This devil-woman knew it better than the rest.

"Listen to what I'm saying," she said. "If you're not interested, we can talk about politics."

"It can't be all in cash," I said.

"Some of it will be jewels," Kate went on. "I know what they're worth. You'll have to take my word for it. If you were willing to wait, you'd get a bigger share. That's what I think you ought to do. Take some cash now, then wait until I get away from here and sell the jewels."

"I hate to wait," I said. "We might get separated and I'd have to search all over for you."

She didn't miss the threat, fake though it was. Even if she double-shuffled me I wouldn't hunt her to the ends of the earth because of some shiny stones. If I followed her there would be other reasons. Like to get in bed with her.

Her green eyes snapped at me like pistols. "What are you going to do with jewelry? Wear it?"

I gave her my best shitkicker grin, knowing it would annoy her no end. "Golly no! I mean to sell off the dadburned stuff."

Kate sneered at me, knowing I had her measure and not liking it. These beauties hate to be figured; it takes away from their mystery.

"However did you get to be so lovable?" she asked. "It would be easy to hate you a lot, the way you are, what you are. Oh, what's the use of talking to a man like you."

"How much cash will there be?" The jewelry would be fine but not that easy to sell at a fair price. Any dealer I came to with jewels would know they hadn't belonged to my grandmother no matter what sort of yarn I spun. I wondered if Kate would give me a bill of sale. Probably not. Anyway, I might have to show it to some sheriff, and if it went that far other things might be resurrected. So I'd have to go where the city burglars go.

"A third of your share will be cash," Kate said, and looked surprised when there was no argument from me. I knew she was hating herself for not having said a quarter. For a woman like Kate hating herself must have come as a shock; she knew she was the cat's ass. She was, and more.

I had a drink to celebrate the money I wasn't sure of. I tried to pour one for her, but she snatched the bottle away from me. Independent, that was my lovely Kate. She knocked it back like a cowhand at the end of a three-month trail drive.

"How does it feel to take money from a woman?" she said, showing me what the chair was getting and I wasn't.

"Not easy," I said. I had a few other things to say and would have said them if Con Flannery hadn't come in. The big Irishman didn't just come in. The door banged open and he filled the doorframe like a man of destiny in a full-length portrait; and it was just as well that he hadn't caught us doing it in Callahan's bed.

He wasn't like me. He didn't like the way his daughter was straddling that chair. "What are you doing here?" he demanded. Flannery didn't talk to people. He asked hard questions and demanded answers.

I could see why there was trouble between them, always would be while both lived. They were too much alike, and that's bad for fathers and daughters. There was no give, no tenderness, as there ought to be. Their lives were being wasted in a contest of wills.

"I asked you a question, Katie," Flannery said, feet planted like a man on a rolling deck.

"It's none of your fucking business," the man's daughter said, standing up to face him, sliding her hand into the side pocket of her skirt at the same time. I thought

117

the skirt sagged a little on the right side. Probably an ivory-handled .32. No pearl grips for this girl. Cheap and flashy, no class. Kate had class and I hoped she wouldn't shoot her father to prove it.

Flannery saw the movement toward the hideaway pistol, but that wasn't what stopped him from belting her. A fierce love seemed to vibrate between them; too late ever to be put into words. A shame the way things go.

Flannery stood aside and told her to get out. Kate approached him warily, her hand still holding the gun we couldn't see.

"Not because you say so," she said, and then she was gone and I was faced with a father's righteous wrath. I thought I was, but all Flannery did was stare at me for about half a minute. A long 30 seconds. Then, turning away, he said, "I still don't know what to make of you. I'll have to think about it some more."

I heard the Flannerys riding away.

ELEVEN

Calvin came back sooner than I expected, and he came back dead, roped across the saddle of my horse and covered with my blanket. As soon as I saw my horse I knew Calvin's body was under that blanket. Three Arizona Rangers brought him in, early in the morning, when I was coming back from breakfast. I got to the jail before they did and waited for them. Their starred badges glittered in the sunlight, and they took no heed of the people who came out to stare at the corpse of the orphaned boy who would never get to be rich and famous like Brady or Gates. I felt my gut turning to lead as they came closer.

They got down and hitched their animals at the jail post. McLandress was hurrying down the street on fat legs, puffing in his eagerness to get in a few licks at me. Right then I couldn't find any reason to fault McLandress. There was nothing he could say about me that I wasn't saying to myself. I had got a boy killed, a poor kid who had nothing to do with any of it, and it was no comfort to wish it had been me instead of him.

Two of the Rangers were somewhere in their late twenties; their boss was about 40, long faced, wind burned, and he had the confident, settled look of a man who knew his business. Without the Ranger badge he could be taken for a cattle buyer or the foreman of a big spread. He moved slowly but not awkwardly: a man who saved his energy. He had big hands, and the handle of his short-barreled Colt .45 hadn't come from the factory. It was bigger than usual and curved back so it filled his hand in just the right way. The other Rangers had nothing remarkable about them.

"I'm Captain Wilkes, Arizona Rangers. I got a dead boy here. Where's Callahan?" The Ranger Captain didn't waste words, and he didn't jerk his thumb toward the corpse.

I told him who I was and he nodded.

"My men, Clagett and Lavery," he said.

I got nods from them.

"You know who he is?" Wilkes asked, lifting the end of the blanket from Calvin's face. He had been shot through the right eye. The other eye was open and the blood on his face had dried. I guessed he had been shot more than once, but I couldn't see the wounds. The rope—my rope—that held his wrists and ankles together went under my horse's belly. My horse whickered at me, nervous among strangers, nervous because of Calvin.

"Calvin Beamer," I said as Wilkes covered the dead face again. "Worked around the jail, the livery, got no family. Where did you find him?"

McLandress got there and let out everything he had been holding back for so long. "Arrest this man, sir. I demand that you arrest this man. He goes by the name of Saddler. Don't be too sure of that. Callahan, that's the Marshal, appointed him deputy without authority. Now he refuses to quit the jail, quit the job. He's holding office illegally. He's been threatening us with guns and he burned and maimed a man—arrest him right now."

Wilkes had clear gray eyes and they moved from me to McLandress, taking in his bulk and his mottled face. McLandress's face grew redder under the Ranger's casual gaze. There was so much the fat banker wanted to say. He wanted to get Callahan and me at the same time. He started up again, as if Wilkes hadn't heard everything he'd said.

"Be quiet, mister," Wilkes said. "The Governor can yell at me, nobody else. Anything you have to say I'll listen to later. Right now I'm going to talk to the Deputy and see what's what. So keep a lid on it, mister, you'll get your chance. Everybody will."

McLandress shut up but he didn't go away. Wilkes turned back to me. "You won't be needing that badge and rifle, Deputy. We're taking over from here on in. The Governor got a report there's big trouble fixing to cut loose down here. We're here to see it doesn't. Suppose you tell me what you know."

McLandress stood there, red faced with anger, while I told my side of it. I told Wilkes most of the truth, all the truth he needed to know. He grunted and here and there prompted me with a question. McLandress cut in when I told about Dorfman and the fight in the jail.

"You're saying this Dorfman didn't try to kill Deputy Saddler?" Wilkes said, eyeing the banker with natural dislike. He managed not to show too much of it.

McLandress blustered, repeating himself. "Mr. Dorfman was acting for the town," he said. "The Judge read the law and Saddler refused to listen. What Dorfman did was not attempted murder. Dorfman would have been the new marshal. In a way, that made him the legal marshal."

"Don't get legal, mister," Wilkes said, cutting off the banker's flow of words. "All that's for the courts to decide." He paused. "If it gets that far. It seems to me the Deputy had a right to defend himself. If you wanted law, you should have waited for the law."

I had been thinking about that. "You mind telling me how you got here so fast?" I asked. "The boy there couldn't have reached the telegraph line."

Wilkes hadn't been against me a moment before. He still wasn't but his voice got hard. Arizona Rangers, as good or better than the more famous Texas boys, don't think much of local law, crooked or honest.

"The Governor doesn't confide in me, Saddler," he said with a tight, faint smile. "He gives orders, I take them. You ought to be glad I'm here."

"Glad enough," I said honestly. "No offense. You won't be able to stop Ballard with two men. Ten Rangers wouldn't be enough."

"I got men on the way," Wilkes said. "We'll keep the peace here. If you want the boy, you can have him. If not . . . I guess the town."

I said I'd look after him. "How often was he shot?" I asked.

"Four times," Wilkes said. "One in the head, three in the body. We found him a day's ride from here, dead but the rigor had worn off. So he was shot long before we came on him. I have to say this, Saddler. You got that boy killed. No more killing is going to happen here. Now gather up your stuff and see to the boy. We're taking over the jail. This town is under Ranger law from now on. You got any objections?"

I knew Danziger was watching from the hotel window. "Sure I have—Jarvis!"

They all went for their guns at the same time. Jarvis was faster than the others, but the other two were good boys. But I had the drop and I used it. I drew and fired and killed Jarvis with a bullet in the heart while his gun was just clearing leather. He staggered back, the gun dropping from his hand, his other hand reaching up to his heart and not making it. Getting the drop was what counted. I had talked them along, seeing them relax as the talk went on.

I fired the next bullet into the man beside Jarvis and

didn't wait for him to drop or die before I fired again. I gave him two and put two more in the other man. They'd hadn't fired a single shot, not even a close miss. The horses jerked away from the rack and one broke loose, heels kicking in fright.

I was down to one bullet in the chamber when Lattigo cut loose from the hotel window, jetting bullets at me, splintering porch wood and causing McLandress to scream like a woman. He was on his belly in the dust with his hands pressed over his face, begging not to be shot. I grabbed up the rifle and ran to the end of the porch and dived under the rail and came up rolling in the alley with Lattigo's bullets chasing me. I crawled up on the porch of the next building, and Lattigo blasted at me with his handgun. Bullets chipped the chairs on the porch, threw chips all around me, but I kept going. I got off the porch and lay under the overhang and reloaded the Colt. I knew he was reloading the rifle. There was yelling up at the hotel window and then it got quiet.

Lattigo's next rifle bullet gouged the heel of my boot without knocking it off. I threw three bullets his way to give me time to get to better cover. I got behind a pile of crates in front of the general store and his return fire didn't do any harm. There was no way to rush the hotel without getting killed. Lattigo would drop me before I ran three yards. I looked up and down the sidewalk wondering if one of the good townspeople might be ready to collect a reward by shooting me in the back. McLandress wouldn't do it. Gunning any man wouldn't come into his thick, righteous head. About Casey, the saloon keeper, I wasn't so sure. If he got rid of me he would earn Danziger's gratitude, for what it was worth, and he would get rid of Callahan, too. Getting shot in the back was something I had to risk.

Bullets tore into crates and I stayed where I was. Danziger wasn't shooting, not yet. A good chance he wouldn't join in. Lattigo was the one to get. He had already lost his life when he fired at me for the first time.

123

And I had to get him fast, then make preparations for the other men Jarvis had said were heading for town. I counted Lattigo's bullets when he cut loose again. He blasted without taking much aim. While he was reloading, I spotted a stack of new blankets lying behind the piled up crates. I picked it up and threw it. It didn't look anything like a man, but it was movement and Lattigo caught it on the fly. I fired while I ran and there was no return fire. Then I was down the street and halfway across it when Lattigo fired the bullets he had loaded. I knew he hadn't loaded all the way, not unless he was the fastest loader who had ever lived. Bullets kicked up dust, but I was down and away from him, and the angle for accurate shooting was bad. I fired at him when he leaned out, and he ducked back.

Now I was in a place where I couldn't see him and he couldn't see me. No one was at the windows or doors on the far side of the street. An alley ran between the hotel and the bank, but I stayed out of it. I didn't know Lattigo or how he worked. He was pretty good. I stayed where I was, to the side of the hotel, away from the big twin window, and waited for him to come to me. Time was on my side. Maybe it was. I didn't do anything when I heard the back door banging. There was no way to figure it. You could bang a door to make the other shooter think you had gone out that way. You could bang it and still go. I didn't hear any more noise after the door banged.

I knew Lattigo's horse was at the livery, but there were two dead men's horses still hitched to the jail rack. My horse stood fretting with the body still on it. Lattigo, unless he had gone out the back way, would have to make a break for the horses at the jail. He knew he couldn't give up. No jail for him. He was a professional gunman and knew how the game worked; knew I would shoot him in the back, kill him unarmed, if I got the chance.

I knew he could be getting away, that was the gamble. I could see the stable but I was a long way from it. He could snag a horse and boom out bareback, and at that distance there wasn't much hope of hitting a moving target. No matter. I'd go after him when I finished killing Danizger. They hadn't killed the boy, hadn't shattered his body with bullets, but they had to die for it. Somebody had to pay for poor dumb book-reading Calvin. If they didn't my whiskey would always have a bad taste.

By now most of my anger had gone away; but there was enough left to be merciless. Just then Lattigo came out the hotel door like a cannon ball. He dived into the street and came up blasting with the rifle, his head swiveling this way and that. He was backing away, the rifle ready, and he was turning to break into a run when he saw me with the stock of the Winchester jammed hard against my shoulder. God! it was good to kill that man. I was ready but still I fired faster than I had to. The first bullet ripped through his heart, and I shot him three times while he was falling. I jacked another shell and made myself stop. There was nothing to shoot at—he was meat!

I walked into the street and Danziger could have shot me from the window if he had the nerve. Lattigo was so dead blue flies buzzed in his leaking blood. Then I turned and looked up at Danziger's window. The window shade flapped against the bullet-shattered window frame. I wasn't watching my back anymore. Casey wouldn't try it now. I went in and the lobby was empty, dusty, flyblown, silent. On the desk the inkwell was spilled; the banging of the back door might have been the clerk getting out fast.

I went up and the door to Danziger's room was open partway. I stood to one side and poked it open all the way with the rifle barrel. At first I saw nothing and then I heard a snuffling sound under the bed. On the dresser Danziger's liquor case was split, broken by a ricocheting bullet. I raised the rifle and said, "Crawl out, Danziger. Crawl out or get killed where you are."

Nothing happened until the snuffling sound began again. I fired a bullet into the floor beside the bed.

Danziger yelled and came crawling out. They had cleaned the room for his arrival, but they hadn't swept under the bed, Danziger, the man who had dinner with the rich and powerful, was covered with lint and dust. It was in his crinkly hair and in his eyebrows. His nightshirt was torn where he had snagged it on some metal part of the bed in his hurry to get under it. His old man's rickety legs had blue veins like cords in the calf. There hadn't been time to get shaved or do anything before the shooting started.

Spittle ran from the corners of Danziger's loose mouth. "Don't kill me, please don't shoot. I told you I didn't want to be part of this. Ballard said—"

I raised the rifle and his body sagged even more. Danziger wanted to turn his back to the bullet. The son of a bitch wanted to turn his back. That's what he was mumbling, and he was turning when I lowered the rifle. No, I thought, this wasn't the way to do it. A quick clean bullet in the back of the head is better than most of us deserve. When the bullet strikes, the instant it smashes the skull, that's all there is. That's what the doctors say: no fading of the light. Bang! you're dead. I wasn't about to let Danziger off so easy, and I didn't give a shit how he got into it. How can a man be so scared that he starts something that goes along until a boy is murdered?

"Turn around," I said, grinning at him, enjoying his fear. Piss ran down his leg and made a pool on the floor. "People keep telling me I'm not the law, so I'm going to prove I am—I'm going to hang you, Danziger. If the Judge was legal enough to read me out of office, he can sentence you to hang. You're under arrest for murder, the murder of Calvin Beamer. Maybe there's a lawyer here that will defend you. You're a lawyer—you can do it. There's the door."

Danziger stepped out of the pool of piss. He still looked sick, but some of the fright had passed, and I could almost hear his crafty brain working again. But he was wrong, dead wrong, about thinking his way out of this. I wanted word of Danziger's trial and hanging to get out, spread far and wide, as far as saloon talk and newspapers could carry it. If it reached Ballard before he started, it might keep him from coming. I didn't think it would. But nothing would be lost except Danziger's dirty life.

"My clothes—" he started to say as the fear faded even more. It wouldn't have faded at all if he had known me better. He would have begged for a bullet and probably would when the noose hung over him.

I grabbed him and shoved him toward the door. "You'll go as you are. Let the town see how big a big man looks in a pissy nightshirt. We'll go down and you can make a speech. Tell them about reopening the mines— they'll want to hear that."

The street was filled with people, but it might have been empty, everything was so quiet. They must have thought Danziger had died when I fired the shot into the bed. Lined along the sidewalk, their faces looked like faces in old photographs, stiff and unsmiling, waiting for the photographer to squeeze the bulb. McLandress had gathered up some of his dignity and was waiting with the rest. His black suit was gray from the dust in the street. My horse came down the street when he saw me, still carrying the body.

I shoved Danziger into the middle of the street and he stood blinking in the sun. Gray hairs glittered in the ginger stubble on his chin. A sort of movement, an easing of tension, seemed to ripple through the people on the sidewalks. It stopped and there wasn't a sound.

I pointed at McLandress and the stable man Bush. "You and you, take the boy off my horse and do it gently. Lay him on the blanket and stand ready." I didn't have to raise my voice in all that silence. "There's going to be a funeral in this town and you're all going to attend. Hide from it and I'll drag you out. You're going to walk behind this boy's coffin and you're going to bow your heads and sing hymns. You're going to kick in the money for a real stone marker for Calvin Beamer. He wanted to be remembered."

An elderly woman spoke up from the front of the crowd. "We didn't kill him, Mr. Saddler. You don't have to drag me to his funeral. But I'll go. That doesn't say we had anything to do with this."

"Some of your men killed him, helped to kill him by standing by when this—this thing here"—I shoved Danziger again and he fell to his knees—"promised you money and that's all you could see. You knew God-damned well he was wrong, what he was trying to do with the Flannery girl. And don't tell me you sided with him because of Ballard. Ballard wasn't your first thought —it was the money. Take a good look at him now. Doesn't look so important, does he?"

The old man who cooked my meals spat close to Danziger's bare feet. "What're you fixing to do with him, Deputy? Turn him over to the law?" The old man grinned. "I forgot—that's you!"

I said, "What I'm fixing to do is put him on trial for murder. Trial starts right after the funeral. Danziger gave a party for you good people, now you'll give one for him. In the ballroom. Like I said about the funeral, everybody is invited."

The old man came forward and pointed to my rifle. "I'd be glad to lock him up for you. So's you can get on with the burying."

I gave the old man my rifle. "Don't kill him unless you have to."

After that I stood by while they took Calvin's bullet-wrecked body to the lumber man's laying-out room, a long high room behind his yard office. Five or six new coffins were stacked against the wall, all plain pine boxes without handles. "That one," I said, pointing to a bigger coffin standing by itself on a work bench. This one was made of dark wood and varnished to a gloss.

"That one's made special for Mr. Dirksen who is dying out on his ranch," the lumber man said.

"You can make another one," I said. "That one for the boy—the town will pay. Get on with it, no more talk."

There wasn't much laying out to be done on Calvin. They put him in the coffin and I took a last look at him. Before they screwed down the lid I sent the stable man to get the boy's well-thumbed book on rich and famous businessmen. I folded his hands around the damn fool book in place of a Bible. He didn't need it. He hadn't done anything to keep him out of wherever it was he was going—had gone.

"All right," I said.

Then the hearse took him out to the cemetery and we all walked behind it. Lattigo, still lying in the street, didn't get any attention. It was Calvin's big day, one they would always remember if only for the events that had brought it about. I saw Laurie in the crowd trying to push her way through the women so she could get close to me. She reached me and whispered as she walked along, eyes downcast.

"I heard what you said just now," she said. "Does that mean you won't be coming with me? I'm sorry about the boy, but I have to think about me. Just this morning my father was saying he'd better send me away. You know about that. So what's holding you back? You've done what you can and it's no use. Please give me an answer so I'll know."

Her father was looking our way with a puzzled look on his face. "I'll tell you sure after Danziger's trial," I said. "I won't let you down. You'll know in time."

Laurie, looking nervously in her father's direction, began to fall back with the women.

"You better not let me down," she said.

TWELVE

Danziger was behind bars and the old man was guarding him when I got back to the jail. It hadn't been a bad funeral. I had nothing to say about Calvin, not to the town of Dragoon Wells, and so I was greatly surprised when McLandress came forward and said he hadn't known Calvin except by name, but was sure he had been a good boy and the Lord was sure to forgive him for any small mischief he might have committed. The rest of them, standing on the hillside that ran down from the burying ground, listened with bowed heads.

That done, they shoveled Calvin under for keeps.

On the way back to town, McLandress walked along with me. I didn't tell him to fuck off because he had, in his clumsy way, done his best to say something for the dead boy. We walked in silence for a while. Then he said, "How did you know they weren't Rangers? You called one of them Jarvis, did you know him before?"

"Years ago back in Texas," I said. "Jimmy Dolan's

Saloon in El Paso, a big place, a lot of games going at the same time. I guess Jarvis never did see me. Jarvis was in a game with some hard cases from up north. Something started and Jarvis killed two men. Two shots, two men. He backed out of there before the law showed up. First time I saw two men killed that quick; so I remembered the man who did it. People told me who he was."

McLandress said, "But how did you know he hadn't joined the Rangers in the years since then? Plenty of wild boys turn about and become lawmen."

I grinned at the fat banker. "Jarvis did too many killings in those years. The Rangers check back on all the men that want to join. They don't do things like they do here."

McLandress was worried again. But he had nerve enough to say, "Maybe you're just as bad as he was."

"No, Banker," I said. "I'm no killer. You mean the way I gunned down Jarvis and his men. I got the drop, they weren't expecting it. What would you have tried to do—put them in jail?"

McLandress considered the question. "They wouldn't let you do that."

"Not likely," I said.

"Would you have . . . if you could?"

"No, Banker. Not after what they did to the boy. I figured they met him on the road and seeing their badges he talked too much. Maybe asked for their help. They killed him and brought the body back so they'd look like lawmen."

The banker's daughter, the lovely Laurie, hurried to hear what we were talking about. I guess she thought I was selling her out to her old man. Trying to match our short steps, she said, "That was a perfectly lovely funeral, don't you think so, Mr. Saddler. Father, you were very moving, the nice way you spoke."

"Hush up," McLandress snorted. "Can't you see we're talking."

"What about, Papa?" Laurie said, trying to link her arm with his. It was like a vine trying to grow up the side of a boulder.

"Town business, girl," McLandress said, disengaging her arm and telling her to go walk with the women.

"Be seeing you now, Mr. Saddler," Laurie called back to me.

"These terrible things, I don't know what to make of them," McLandress started off, fumbling for the right words. "All the things you said about Danziger and Ballard, they're hard to believe. You were a stranger to us—why should we have believed you?"

We were nearly back to town, passing the place where Callahan had broken his legs, where it all started. "You believe me now, Mr. McLandress?"

"I saw that dead boy," McLandress said. "It's funny. Nothing else you said made any difference. It took the boy to change that."

"And if Calvin hadn't been killed? What then?"

"I don't know. I knew you were right and Danziger was wrong. If the boy hadn't been killed I probably would have stayed on Danziger's side. The Flannery girl wasn't all that important."

"What about now?"

"You want an honest answer, I'll give you one. I wish she'd go away from this town. With her gone Ballard wouldn't burn us out. But we can't make her go; so Ballard will think we had a hand in keeping her here. So he'll burn the town or try to. Would you say that's right, Deputy?"

This was the first time McLandress had called me Deputy since the trouble began. "He'll try it," I said. "I'm still asking for your help. You sound like you're ready to give it."

McLandress looked at me. "There's an old and very good rule in business, Deputy. Cut your losses, don't invest any more capital when you're losing. That's what we've been doing with Danziger, and it's time we stopped. We'll help you because it's the sensible thing to do."

You could hardly call that a heart-warming declaration, but it was honest. It was a banker's answer and I liked it fine.

We were in front of the jail and we looked at each other, two men who could never be friends. McLandress had a bulldog jaw underneath the fat put there by thousands of big dinners, but I knew he would keep his word once he gave it. That was the reasonable way to look at it. He might change his mind if Ballard rode into town on a donkey waving an olive branch and strewing $1,000 bills. And that, I was reasonably sure, was not about to happen. So poor old Calvin had done some good after all.

"I'll bring Danziger down to the hotel," I said. "That man has to hang."

"You want a suggestion, Mr. Saddler?"

"I'll listen."

McLandress said, "Don't keep telling people what to do. This is our town and we'll decide if Danziger is to hang." And with that he stumped on down to the hotel.

Danziger was still in his nightshirt and I asked the old man to fetch his clothes. Danziger gripped the bars of his cell, as if testing their strength. "You really mean to go through with this, Saddler?"

"That's the idea." I sat down and poured a drink. Danziger looked at the bottle and licked his lips. "No," I said. Then I changed my mind and filled a glass for him. He bolted the whiskey and held out his glass again. I took it and put it on the desk.

With whiskey in him, Danziger got a little cockier. "You know what you're doing is wrong, Saddler. I killed nobody, never carried a gun in my life."

I had another drink. "You brought Jarvis here."

"That was to prevent killing, not to start it," Danziger said. "You were supposed to get out; they were supposed to take over. I don't know why they had to kill the boy.

133

Maybe he tried to run."

"Calvin had no sense," I said. "There's nothing to talk about, not a thing. I told you to back off and you kept on coming. Now you're going. I'll hang you myself, I'm the law."

I got up and gave Danziger another drink. I wanted him to think about the things he'd be missing on the other side. This was a man who lived for the good things in life, but I knew he didn't enjoy them like a normal man. Danziger was a glutton for whiskey and rich food. He loved the appearance of comfort more than comfort itself.

"You're wrong if you think Ballard will get here in time," I said. What I did next was just for show. I reached into my pocket, which was full of cartridges, and took one out and held it up between thumb and forefinger. I turned the stubby brass cylinder before I dropped it in my lefthand shirt pocket. "That one is for you," I said. "That pocket is empty except for that bullet. I'll save that one for last. I'd save that one for you even if I had to face torture by not using it on myself."

"You're crazy," Danziger said. "You've been acting crazy all along. You won't take money and you won't run. That makes you crazy. Say what you want. Maybe I tried to buy you too cheap. No more bluffing, not now. Name a price and I'll meet it. How much?"

"You're wasting your time." When we weren't talking the big wooden clock on the wall made a loud tick. "Don't waste too much—you don't have much. You'll be dead in less than two hours." I knew what I wanted from Danziger, but I wanted to be sure of getting the truth. Faced with certain death, another man would be ready to tell the truth. It wasn't that simple with Danziger. Lying was natural as breathing to this man, and it was doubtful if he ever told the whole truth in his life. You would almost have to see and hear this man, to know what I'm talking about. No matter what, he would try to hold something back.

"There has to be something," Danziger said, sweat dribbling from his crinkly hair. In his face a muscle twitched that hadn't twitched before. The clock ticked and I heard the old man coming back with the clothes.

He came in and slung the clothes over the back of a chair. He hawked up a gob when he looked at Danziger but spat in the stove instead of on the floor. I told him to pour himself a drink.

"What's your name?" I asked him. "Sorry but I never did hear it."

He said they called him Dad Switzer and we said how-do, introduced at last. "You want me to start tying the rope?" he said.

"Have it ready," I said. "Tell McLandress I'll be there in a few minutes.

I pushed the clothes and boots through the bars of the cell, and when Danziger finished dressing ten minutes were left. I held up the key but didn't put it in the lock. "I want you to listen to me, Danziger. You get one chance to talk, tell me everything you know. One chance, then you hang. Convince yourself what I'm saying is the truth. There's no one here to help you, no politicians, no rich men, no Ballard. Keep it simple. What's Ballard going to do?"

Danziger started to tie his ribbon tie, but it would have felt too much like a rope. He threw it away and took hold of the bars again. "You'll let me go free if I give you what you want?"

I shook my head. "Not a chance. You can't murder a boy and walk away from it. The trade is, information for life in jail. You monkeyed with fake Rangers so you'll go before the Governor's Tribunal. You confess to me, you'll get life."

Danziger pretended to think about it. "That's not such a good trade. That the best you can do?"

I knew the son of a bitch was ready to jump at the chance, and being a lawyer, he knew that anything he told me, without witnesses present, didn't mean a fucking thing. Once he was lodged in the jail in the capital, he would start pulling strings to get out. He would call in every I.O.U. he held on every politician in the Territory. Getting Danziger where I wanted him was like trying to land a big trout with a thin line.

"Take it or leave it," I said.

"What's to say you won't double-cross me? You don't play by any rules."

I smiled, one bad man to another. "You can't give me money if you're dead. That's it, Danziger. I want something to ease my conscience for not hanging you. I'm not like you, I'm an honest crook."

Danziger smiled nervously, but he did smile. I guess he no longer saw the noose hanging over him. "Why not just settle for the money. Name a price, I'll get what you want."

I said no. It had to be jail. The clock began to whir as its metal insides got ready to chime the hour. "The hell with any more talk, let's go," I said.

"Suppose they find me guilty?"

"They will, but it's up to me to hang you. I'll get the Judge to set the time for tomorrow morning. We'll be long gone by then."

Danziger gulped and I hoped the habit of lying wasn't so deeply ingrained that it was impossible for him to tell the truth. "No more fake Rangers will be coming. Jarvis was all. If Ballard doesn't hear from me by tomorrow he'll be on his way. Jarvis was the last hope of doing it the easy way. Ballard will be here the day after tomorrow, maybe sometime late tomorrow if he pushes it."

It was my turn to be surprised, though I didn't show it. "Then he's already in the Territory. No other way he could get here that fast."

"Ballard figured he'd be spotted if he had led a big party across the border at the same time. That was smart, he probably would. Especially a big party of Mexicans. That would bring out the army in force. So he's been bringing them across five or ten at a time. At night, no show of force, no invasion. The plan was to make camp in a deep canyon not much more than a day south of here. You think you're doing me a favor. I'm doing you just as big a one. You won't be here when Ballard comes. He'll be mad and murderous, no more chance of a pardon after this. So all bets will be off. This will be the last time he ever crosses that border and he'll want people to remember it. You know what he said to me? He said, 'If it goes wrong and I have to come, Dragoon Wells will be just a name on a map.'"

I wanted to shoot Danziger in the mouth. Instead, I asked how many men Ballard had.

"I don't know that, can only guess," Danziger said. "Seventy-five is a good guess. Could even be more."

Jesus Christ! And every one of them a professional killer, men who had learned their grisly trade in regular and bandit armies. Mostly they'd be Mexicans but some Americans too. Americans rode with the Mexicans only by proving they could be worse than the Mexicans.

I unlocked the door for Danziger, and he said, "I'd like to be gone from this place." He didn't mean the jail but the town. He'd be gone all right, but not the way he intended. He was going to keep Calvin company for all time, because there was nothing I could think of that would cause me to turn him over to the Territorial Law, allow him to go on living. If I could get Ballard, then I'd get him; Danziger was here and he had to go first. I can't say I even hated the man. I was past that. He was filth that had to be washed away, a shithouse bucket that had to be emptied. A double cross? You bet it was. But of course Danziger knew none of that when I marched him down to the hotel at the point of my rifle. People who couldn't get into the ballroom lined the sidewalks to watch Danziger going to face justice. Lattigo's body had been taken away; there was a bloody patch where he had fallen. By now everyone knew the story—McLandress's doing—and no kind faces were turned toward old Earl. They liked him less when they saw he wasn't too repentant. Danziger thought that once again he had wormed his way out of a tight place. There was no point in telling him that he was walking to his death, with only a short layover in the make-do courtroom.

Why did I bother to go through with what I was doing? Stand him in front of a judge and jury and let them deal with him? Truth to tell, I didn't much care about the law, and still don't. My real intention was to put some backbone into these people for the fight that lay ahead. This was their town and I wanted them to remember it. Doing away with Danziger was the first step toward giving them back their self-respect. Once men have that they will fight to hell and gone.

What I had to do next was get the Flannerys to join in. There was no beating Ballard without them. How I was going to persuade them—persuade old Con, the only one who mattered—was still a question. As for Laurie there was nothing more to decide. In the years to come I would want to kick himself; there was no help for it—she would have to go without me. I would tell her the best way to do it, tell her to drop the idea of Havana or Mexico City. Go to New York and brazen it out, I'd tell her. Her old man wouldn't call in the law. It was a hard thing to have to do, to give her up. Did I love her? That's too complicated to answer. I don't stay with women for very long, or maybe it's the other way around. I don't have much to do with the faint-hearted ones; so there is no hard feeling when it's over. Women like that are always in need of a change of men, and I'm the same way about women. If you think it odd for a man to think about women on the way to a hanging that's how it was. But life would go on after Earl Danziger was dead. Fact is, life would be a tiny bit better for his passing.

Danziger balked some when he got his first look at the noose dangling from the hay hoist at the livery stable. It was a simple way of doing it. Danziger would walk, or be carried, up to the hayloft to have his necktie fitted. Then he'd be thrown out the door. There was a good drop, more than enough to swing him off in style. I didn't mind if he choked a bit when he ran out of rope.

Danziger looked away from the rope, his eyes begging for reassurance. He got a nod from me. I was done with lying to the sneaky son of a bitch. "Go in," I said.

They were waiting, all that could squeeze into the dusty old ballroom. Danziger had more people at this party than at the first one. People were there I hadn't seen before—but no Flannerys. I guessed Con Flannery had a spy in town; if so, old Con would know the whole story by now. On a fast horse it wasn't that far to the ranch.

The Judge's bench was the bandstand with a table and chair placed in the middle of it. Someone had hung a flag on the back wall, and the Judge was already in his chair with a Bible and the Laws of Arizona Territory in front of him. I could tell he'd fortified himself with a couple of big drinks, but that was all. The Judge had that normal, sober look that some drunks have in the first half of the day. He would do just fine.

McLandress and 11 men sat behind a trestle table to one side of the bench, and most of them I'd seen before. Bush the stable keeper was one of them. McLandress came over when I brought Danziger in.

"There's no lawyer for him. Wilcox said he was too sick to defend him."

Even then, Danziger had to show off. "That's all right, Mr. McLandress. There's not going to be any trial here."

The banker's eyes jumped to me. "What's he talking about?"

I looked straight at Danziger so there could be no mistake. "I don't know," I said. "It's got nothing to do with me."

Danziger swayed on his feet as if he had been punched hard and had just enough strength left to keep from falling. The color drained from his face and his slack mouth worked convulsively. "You dirty bastard—you lied to me!" Then he came at me with both hands, but

139

McLandress drove him away with his bulk and turned to stare at me again.

"He's crazy with fear," I said. "He'll say anything."

Maybe McLandress believed me. It hardly mattered. He wrestled Danziger into a chair on the other side of the bench, facing the jury table, and warned him to stay there or he'd be tied. When all that was done, he came back to me.

"You have to prosecute. There's nobody else."

I hadn't thought much about that. All I know about the law is not to get caught by it. I nodded and that made me a prosecutor.

The Judge liked having a courtroom to preside over. He wiped his spectacles and steadied them on his long nose. "I declare this court in session," he said. "This court, in special session, will hear the charge against Earl Danziger, the charge being murder, the murder of Calvin Beamer. You will act as prosecutor, Mr. Saddler?"

I stood up and said I would.

The Judge glanced over at Danziger. "And who will represent the defendant?"

Danziger got up too. "I will."

"Your honor," the Judge said.

Danziger said, "I will, your honor."

"Proceed," the Judge said, leaning back in his hair chair.

I kept to the facts. I told about sending Calvin to the telegraph line, the way he came back, the gunfight with Jarvis and his gunmen, the killing of Lattigo after he had opened fire on me from the window of Danziger's room. I testified that Danziger had confessed his part in the killing of Calvin Beamer.

Danziger jumped to his feet. "I did no such thing, your honor. This man solicited a bribe from me."

The Judge, glaring at Danziger, pounded the tabletop for silence. "Sit down, Mr. Danziger, you'll get your chance."

Then the Judge peered down at me. "Is that the

conclusion of your testimony, Mr. Saddler?"

I said it was and the Judge said I could make my closing remarks later. "All right, Mr. Danziger," he said.

Danziger walked up in front of the bench and looked around for something to lean on. Not finding it, he stood up as straight as he could. "With due respect, your honor, I submit that this court has no jurisdiction in this case. This being a Territory and not a State, this trial should properly be held in front of the Governor's Tribunal."

"Why is that?" the Judge wanted to know.

"Because Territorial Law states that any crime against the sovereignty of the Territory takes precedence over all lesser crimes. That includes homicide, your honor. I hereby plead guilty to the charge of conspiracy to cause three men to impersonate Territorial peace officers."

"I cannot accept your plea, Mr. Danziger," the Judge said. The charge here is murder. We have only Mr. Saddler's word that the three men he killed were not real peace officers."

Danziger gaped. "But you just admitted his testimony."

"We heard his testimony, Mr. Danziger. The jury must decide what to do with it."

"But Saddler was telling the truth. The three men he killed were hired gunmen. I sent for them, sent a man to instruct them to pose as Arizona Rangers. That's what Saddler said, I'm saying it too. That makes it a matter for the Tribunal."

The Judge leaned forward in his chair. "This court is not inclined to believe Mr. Saddler's testimony. Not only is he the prosecutor in this case, he is also a hostile witness and shall be characterized accordingly."

"But he was telling the truth, your honor."

"The jury must decide that. At the moment I must decide whether there is a compelling reason why this trial should not continue. I am afraid that Mr. Saddler's testimony is not enough." The Judge cleared his throat.

"And neither is yours, Mr. Danziger. Obviously, it would be to your advantage to have this trial stopped. Therefore, since there is no reliable testimony"—I swear the Judge winked at me—"this trial for murder will continue. You may proceed, Mr. Danziger."

"Proceed!" Danziger was indignant. "This entire proceeding is irregular, your honor. The prosecutor is the principal witness against me. I demand a proper trial."

"No," the Judge said with no legal jargon added.

"I was given no opportunity to participate in the selection of the jury."

"Do you object to certain members of the jury? If so, I will take that under consideration, Mr. Danziger. You don't, then we will proceed. Your objections are overruled. Territorial Law states that certain formalities may be dispensed with when there is a state of emergency. One exists here, I believe. You will be seated, Mr. Danziger while Mr. Saddler makes his closing address to the jury. You may do that, Mr. Saddler."

Once again, I kept it short, and there was no legal language used. Danziger had convicted himself out of his own mouth, in his attempt to get the trial moved to the capital, and for once the jury members were hearing law talk they could understand. I said Danziger hadn't murdered the boy; that a man didn't have to pull the trigger to kill another human being. I was out of bounds when I told them they had to hang Danziger because this was their town and they had the say in it. No objection came from Danziger and the Judge didn't steer me back into narrow legal channels.

"It's up to you," I concluded.

I sat down and let Danziger run off at the mouth. He was talking for his life—already lost—and the Judge let him talk. If it had been a jury made up of strangers, he might have bullshitted his way out of it. But he was playing against a stacked deck. Still and all, he wasn't bad. The jury got a rundown on his whole career and all the important men he knew. They got the poverty of his early years; how he slopped hogs, taught himself to read. His old Maw and Paw were so goldarned proud when he got his lawyer's papers after reading law in some small-town attorney's office. Then they got the rest of it: the times he ran for Governor of Texas, the big men he helped get elected. He left out the railroad scandal, then remembered that he had nothing to lose by admitting to his part in it. He thought that was his trump card, the hold Ballard had over him. The threat of jail or death.

"I admit it, gentlemen," he declared. "In my time I have been a venal and wicked man, but I am no killer. Yes, gentlemen, I am guilty of avarice and bribery, but I am innocent of the crime of murder."

McLandress and the others didn't even retire to another room. All they did was put their heads together and whisper. There was a lot of solemn nodding and then McLandress stood up.

"We the jury find the defendant guilty," he said.

The Judge had just finished sentencing Danziger to hang—sentence to be carried out immediately—when a boy burst into the courtroom yelling, "The Flannerys are back! The Flannerys are back!"

THIRTEEN

The Flannerys were at the end of the street, waiting by the stable where Danziger was to hang. They sat on their horses in silence, spread out in a half circle so they wouldn't get in the way. Dangling from the hay hoist, the rope stirred in the hot wind that blew in from the south, and the Flannerys didn't stir when I brought Danziger out, with McLandress and all the others following along.

Before we left the court, I got bottle of whiskey from Casey and told Danziger to drink all he wanted. I watched while he emptied more than half a pint into his belly. Outside he asked for more and I let him drink. After that he walked pretty good, but not too steady. We went down to the hanging place with the whole town behind us.

Danziger got another drink and said, "I got to hand it to you, Saddler. You put one over on me that's never had one put. You think I'm afraid to die, you lousy saddletramp. At least I had a life, not like you. Gambler my asshole! You're just a fucking bum! You know how

144

you're going to die! With nothing but the rags on your back. I'm dying a rich man and nobody's going to get a cent of my money. It's where nobody'll ever find it."

I let him talk. In a few minutes he would sound off no more. I didn't see Kate until we were close to the stable. She was in back of all the Flannerys but this time not sitting sidesaddle and not wearing lady clothes. She had on the range clothes she'd worn on the first night she came to the jail. Her face was drawn and white, but still beautiful. In a way, she should have been out in front of her kin. It was happening because of her, so she should have had a place of prominence right after Danziger.

Danziger saw her too and swept off his hat and nearly fell over making a bow. "Your husband misses you, Mrs. Ballard," he said. "You better hurry back to his bed and board." Danziger bent over laughing and I pulled him to his feet.

Con Flannery sat his big horse like a statue and the Creedmore Sharps was out of its scabbard. All the Flannerys had rifles in their hands.

"I heard you were going to do it and came to watch," Flannery said. "I guess you are."

Danziger was laughing again, about as drunk as he could get. He looked at Kate. "You fair to broke Peyton's back, missus."

Kate's hothead brother, the one named Emmet, started to bring out his gun. My gun was out first. "Try it, sonny," I said. "You can die too."

Hardly turning, Con Flannery backhanded his son across the face, all but knocking him off his horse. Then he looked at me. "We're still waiting."

I pushed Danziger toward the door of the stable. "Wait all you like, it's not being done for you."

Danziger went up the ladder by himself, and give McLandress his due, he climbed up too. Dad Switzer was standing by the open door of the loft and he reached out and grabbed the rope and brought it inside. It's hard to tell about men. Danziger held still while the noose was dropped over his head, then tightened and moved so the knot was behind his left ear. The whiskey had a lot to do with it, but not all of it. He ignored McLandress and Dad and aimed all his badmouthing at me. Some of what he said had truth in it, and you'd think because of that I should have enjoyed the thought of swinging him off. I didn't, and in the end I didn't have to. Suddenly, Danziger stopped talking and his face sagged like an old man going to sleep.

His voice came out in a surprised, "I'm going to die." He turned as if to escape through the open door of the hoist. Dad Switzer tripped him and he went flying out to the end of the rope. His neck cracked like a pistol shot and he was dead.

"I make a nice noose," Dad Switzer said in the same tone he used to praise his flapjacks. McLandress, white faced, didn't say anything. Dad said he would see to the body, and I went down to see what Con Flannery had to say. I was fresh out of reasonable words when I faced him again.

"You in or out?" I said. "There's no more time to waste in talk. If you're out, then get the hell out of this town. And I don't want to hear any more Irish bullshit about how unfriendly these people are. They're ready to stand up to Ballard with what they have. What the fuck are you going to do?"

"We're in," he said, looking at McLandress instead of me. "It's too bad the town has to suffer because of us."

McLandress didn't like to hear his town referred to in a pitying way. "You don't have to stay if you don't want. We can manage without you, Flannery." The banker turned and pointed to Danziger's body while Dad Switzer was still sawing at the rope with a clasp knife. Danziger's body dropped to the street. "We did that," McLandress said. "That's Earl Danziger we just hung. You think that didn't take some nerve."

Flannery spat. "Looked to me like he fell out that door."

McLandress refused to let go the credit. "With our rope around his neck, same thing," he said.

I got into the argument. "Save it for later," I said. "We have to talk about Ballard."

They followed me to the jail and I got out a bottle and poured a drink for Flannery, who took it without a word. I shook the bottle at McLandress and he hesitated before he said yes. Kate went past on her horse and I wondered where she was going. Laurie hadn't turned up at the trial or the hanging, but enough about my two ladies, I decided.

They got grim faced when I told them that Ballard was already on his way to Dragoon Wells. "We have some time," I said. "He may go to the ranch looking for your daughter, Mr. Flannery. Probably not. If he goes to the ranch and finds it deserted he'll burn you out. What about your womenfolk?"

Flannery drank more whiskey. "I sent them back in the hills when I came here. Kate wouldn't go, that's why she's along."

"Girls nowadays," McLandress said, shaking his head at the worry caused to fathers by young females of a certain kind—the kind I like.

"You said a mouthful," Con Flannery said, sliding the bottle to the banker.

I talked and they listened.

"First thing we have to do is keep Ballard from finding out that Danziger is dead. If he hears Danziger is dead he'll figure he talked. If that happens there won't be any way to lead him into a trap. A trap is our only hope. Any hope of getting help from the other ranchers?"

Con Flannery said not a prayer. "They're staying neutral in this. Hoping they won't get burned out too. Like you said before, what you see is what we've got."

"Then it'll have to do," I said. "Ballard won't expect anybody is going to fight him, so we're ahead there. Part of the same surprise. You sure you can talk for all the men in town, Mr. McLandress?"

McLandress was on his second glass of whiskey. "Call me Dougal," he said, making faces at the bite of the whiskey but enjoying it. "I can talk for the men that count. A few will sneak out, so we'd better post guards on the road to the south."

I said, "It's not likely they'll go that way, but we better send men out to watch for Ballard."

Flannery shoved his empty glass away from him. "You know there's always a chance Danziger was lying about the time. Maybe Ballard isn't as close as he said."

Kate Flannery passed the window again. I looked back to her father. "Maybe he hasn't even left Mexico. We don't know, so we have to figure he's right on top of us. Let's get to it."

Outside, McLandress surprised me by saying that he had been a militia major at one time. I knew the kind of officer he'd been, but I needed anything I could get. Flannery was different, a hardbitten man who had bulled his way through the bloodiest war fought on this continent. Flannery and his tough-looking brothers were going to make one hell of a difference. Even so, it was going to take more than courage to beat Ballard. Beat him hell! We'd be lucky if we could give him enough grief to make him head back for the border. If we could do that the town would be safe; an invasion of Arizona was going to get a lot of attention from the army.

We went out to get ready for a battle.

The first thing I did was to have Flannery and McLandress assemble their men in the hotel. Not all the men from the town turned up for the war talk, but the Flannerys were there, looking down their noses with the contempt ranchers have for town dwellers. I made no attempt to lessen the hostility between the two factions. It might make for a better fighting force, one side trying to show up the other. Using the lumber man's thick crayon pencil, I made a map of the town on the wall. I didn't have to rap for attention; their lives depended on it, they didn't have to be told.

I said, "We have to suppose Ballard will come in from the south. No reason why he shouldn't. They're a strong force and won't feel the need to be cautious. Danziger said Ballard is hopping mad. To a crazy man like Ballard that means killing mad. In one way that's good. It could make him careless. But it's going to be bad if we lose. You can't expect any mercy if you lose. Ballard will kill and burn until there's nothing left."

The Flannerys didn't budge, but some of the town men stirred uneasily, and I knew we'd be losing a few more men before Ballard got close to town. That was just as well; I didn't want to post men I couldn't count on. But for the moment the deserters stayed.

"We have to play hell with them, and we have to do it fast. If all we do is beat off an attack, then we're done for. Ballard will split his force and come at us from all sides. They'll bring along all the guns, all the ammunition they need. So we can't let it become a siege."

Bush the stable keeper glanced nervously at Con Flannery. "No offense meant to any man present, but I got a question that has to be asked."

I knew what was coming and it was better to get it out of the way. "Ask it," I said.

Bush said, "Would Ballard attack the town if his wife wasn't here?"

Con Flannery warned his people to be quiet. I was beginning to have respect for this big, bullying man.

"There's still time for her to go north," Bush said, fidgeting under the Irishman's stare. "If she started right now, with a strong escort, her family men, what's to stop her from reaching safety? There's an army post five days north of here. It seems to me Ballard wouldn't dare take his greasers that far north."

All their eyes moved to me. Some of what Bush said was true; it all depended on how close Ballard was to Dragoon Wells. Men were posted well south of town, and so far there was no sign of the approaching force. But it was hilly country south of where we were, and men would be hard to spot, even a large force like this one. My guess was that even if the Flannerys started now they wouldn't have more than half a day's start. Even so, the stable man had a point.

"Mrs. Ballard could do that, ride north with an escort, and there's a chance she could get away with it. There's the other chance that she'll be overtaken if she goes. What isn't a guess is Ballard will burn this town anyway. He's got nothing to lose. They can't hang him twice."

McLandress, the old windbag, sided with me. "No more of that kind of talk. Go on with it, Deputy."

I said, "We have to make sure they come in fast. Men have to be on the south road where Ballard can see them. They are to turn and run when they spot the Mexicans." It was hard to ask for volunteers, men who faced almost certain death. "They'll ride you down, the ones that go. If it's dark when they come you'll have some chance of getting off the road and hope they'll be more interested in the town. But the men who go will be the means of winning this fight."

Dad Switzer pushed his way through to the front. He said, "You remember the time I told you I wasn't afraid of dying because I plan to shoot myself when I get too old to work." Dad Switzer spat. "I just quit working—I'll go. Just don't ask me to run too hard."

Con Flannery gave me a grim smile. "I'd be more use here, but I'll go if you say."

"Not you and not McLandress," I said.

Kate's mean-looking brother said he'd go, but I turned him down too. The oldest of the Flannery brothers, a stooped man with lines of pain his face, said it was all right with him. He said he was sick and a widower, so he didn't care that much. His son, a rangy boy named Phelim, submitted that they might as well keep it in the family. His father, Conor, objected but the boy held firm. "They ain't going to run me down," he said, and we all wished he hadn't said it. He looked fast enough to run off into the dark, if they came in the dark, but there was no hope for his father and Dad Switzer.

I went on with it. "We hope it works and they come in fast fixing to level the town. We let them get about halfway down the street before we open fire. We begin firing at the south end of the street. Really throw lead at them down there. That way they won't try to turn. They'll ride on through to the north end and then turn. Only they won't get that far because of the trenches dug all the way across the street."

Con Flannery, the Civil War veteran, rubbed his face. "You're going to put us in trenches. That won't work, Mr. Saddler."

"Not men in the trenches," I said. "Pine boards at the bottom of the trenches with six-inch nails driven through and pointing up. That's the first trench. In the second and third, cheval-de-frise and rolls of barbwire. Two trenches north and south, coal oil for light."

"Sure," Con Flannery said. "The trenches just the right distance apart so a horse can clear one but not the next one. I saw that done in Virginia, not in a town though. The spikes on the cheval are going to play hell with the horses."

"And men. You land on a spike you don't get up again. The ditches have to be wide and deep, then the top covered with wagon covers stretched tight and anchored with long pegs so they won't pull loose. Then everything is covered with dirt and brushed smooth. It has to look right if they come by day. Won't make any difference at night."

"You got the alleys figured in this?" Flannery asked.

I nodded. "They won't try to get out through the alleys until they find the street completely blocked. To stop them from riding up on the sidewalks and porches and getting by the trenches that way, we have to block everything off with anything that can be moved. They'll have to turn to the alleys to get out."

McLandress wanted to demonstrate that he was as smart as the Irishman. "More cheval-de-frise in the alleys?"

"Coils of barbwire, everything in the stores, any wire you can find. It has to be spread high and loose so there is no way through. The harder they fight to get through, the worse off they'll be. And all the time we'll be pouring lead at them."

"By God! I'm beginning to feel sorry for the bastards," McLandress said, still feeling the effects of the whiskey. "They'll get such a trouncing they'll never come back to this town."

"No," I said.

McLandress lifted his bushy eyebrows. "No!" he echoed.

The Irishman knew what I meant, but didn't say anything. It had to be a slaughter, or as near as slaughter as we could make it. I hoped the men from the town would have the stomach for what had to be done. I figured the Flannerys wouldn't be squeamish.

"No quarter," I said. "That means we kill every man we can, wounded, unarmed, wanting to surrender—no quarter! They wouldn't show us mercy, but that's not the reason. This has to be total war. If too many escape they could come back. I want the name Dragoon Wells to spread fear clear into Mexico."

It's a hellish thing to see what whiskey can do to a banker. Seized by the spirit of killing, McLandress whipped an old Starr .45 revolver from the waistband of his pants and brandished it in the air.

"We'll massacre the greasy bastards! Remember the Alamo!" he yelled.

I went out with Con Flannery, and we were the last to leave. A sour smile twisted his face and his eyes were bright with the anticipation of the fight ahead. He was a strange man, always hard to figure.

"You really think we can do it?" he said.

It would be useless to try to bullshit this hard man. "If

we get lucky," I said.

The man- and horse-killing trenches were more important than anything else, and we got everybody digging and hauling dirt. It was a sight to see McLandress down in a hole digging with the poor men he would have snorted at a few days before. There was plenty of pick and crowbar work mixed in with the digging. In the early days, when Dragoon Wells was an ambitious town, they had dug up the main street and paved it end to end with rocks, then covered everything with a layer or gravel and dirt. Years and poor times had put holes and ruts in it, but it was still rock hard, and the only thing we could be thankful for was that it hadn't been paved.

It was the closest thing to the old frontier spirit that I had seen for a long time. Women and girls kept the coffee coming, and even Casey, the pimping saloonkeeper, was loading buckets of dirt. Over at the lumber yard they were nailing the chevals together, drilling holes in beer barrels from the saloons, malleting round staves into the holes, and then sharpening the points. The cheval-de-frise is one of the most terrible defensive weapons ever invented. No matter how you fall on it you get killed or wounded so badly that it doesn't make any difference. You can't rope it and drag it away because the rope slips off the greased staves. All you can do with a cheval is stay away from it, if you can, or die on it.

All the stores were open and nobody was making any money. Wagons loaded with great rolls of barbwire went up both sides of the streets. When they got to an alley or any space between the buildings, they dumped down rolls or wire and unrolled it. In the alleys rough barriers had been nailed together and the barbwire was coiled and strung across everything. Up and down the street came the sound of shattered glass as the windows that were to serve as firing positions were knocked out. The doors, most of them, were barred or blocked from the inside by furniture, and what wasn't used for that was dragged out to block off the sidewalks.

But everything depended on those three trenches. Four or five would have been better, but there wasn't time for that. The rocks from the street were piled along the sidewalks in front of the firing positions. The thing I feared most was fire; there was nothing that could be done about that, and it was too much to hope that part of the town wouldn't burn. It had to: Ballard would come ready to burn. I knew what Ballard looked like, and hoped I'd get a chance to kill him for Calvin. It was all Ballard's doing from start to finish. He wouldn't be hard to spot. Like all madmen he wasn't a coward and he wouldn't hide in a gully and let the Mexicans do the killing. He'd be right out in front of his private army, already crazy and now crazier because of a woman, and I wondered if Kate considered the many men who were to die because of her. Probably not.

For hours it looked as if we would never get it finished. The main street was like an upturned ants' nest, with the ants running every which way. But the thought of dying makes a man work harder than money ever can. They got the trenches finished and the lumber man's helpers began to drag the chevals over from the yard. Those damn things were our salvation; they gave me a cold feeling just the same. Flannery was down in the first trench setting them up, pressing down on the back spikes so they wouldn't move when men and horses came crashing down to their deaths. Jesus! I could just about hear the screaming of the horses.

Flannery got the first trench finished and moved on to the second while men stretched wagon covers and pegged them taut. They drove the pegs in close to the wide end and began to scatter on dirt, moving it around with brooms, covering everything. A man who was tired or plain clumsy nearly fell into the second trench and would have died if Flannery hadn't yanked him to safety by the collar.

They got the third ditch covered and dusted with dirt. One of the young Flannerys rode back from the edge of town and said it was quiet out there. I had one of them reporting every ten minutes. Dad Switzer and the other two men were out on the road, sitting there with bread and meat and water, not a hearty meal for men under sentence of death.

It was close to dark when we finished. I told McLandress to make sure the town didn't get too lit up. Too much light thrown up into the sky would alert Ballard long before he got close.

Next came the parceling out of guns and ammunition. Some likely looking men had old guns, or no guns, and that had to be changed, a cause for considerable grumbling. I had to take away a cared-for '73 Winchester from a very old man and give it to one of McLandress's tellers, a wiry man who had been in the army in Canada. There was a fair collection of standard weapons, rifles, shotguns and revolvers, but you should have seen some of the others. In that pile of old iron was a .22 caliber "bicycle" pistol, a one-shotter carried by Eastern ladies to discourage rapists from unwheeling them, or however you want to say it. Still, it was a gun and it could kill, provided you put the small caliber in the right place. I took it away from a small boy and gave it to a woman with a rock jaw and a build like a man. Yes, and there were swords and bayonets, pitchforks and sickles, carving knives and a Bowie knife with a broken tip. Nothing was refused, everything was handed out to the most likely fighters. I didn't see Laurie but Kate was all over the place. No one was going to take the .38 Colt Lightning, the fast firing double-action that was belted high around her waist. She had an '86 Winchester and the pockets of her wool shirt bulged with bullets. All the Flannerys had good weapons, all Winchesters except for old Con's Creedmore. The doctor was there with two black bags instead of one, and a basket filled with bandages. I didn't tell him there wouldn't be any doctoring done during the fighting. If it slowed down to that point, we would have lost, or would lose. A few faces were missing, nothing to be done about them, and it was hard to blame them for ducking out, though McLandress, who had been nipping again, cursed them for gutless cowards. The fat banker had turned into a regular fireater, now that he had cast off the starchy skin he had been wearing all his life. He even bellowed at his top sergeant of a wife when she suggested he drink black coffee and not get so excited.

And then, suddenly, we were ready. As ready as we'd ever be—and after that there was nothing to do but wait.

FOURTEEN

Kate had stayed away from me since she had come to town, and that was understandable, given the circumstances. But now it was quiet, and I was sitting alone in the jail, and still there was no sign of her.

Apart from the bank the jail was the strongest building in town, and as a defensive position it couldn't be bettered. That wasn't the idea—we were the attackers. The windows were too narrow to position a lot of men, and it wasn't in the right place. At the first shot far from town I would take my place with the others.

A woman brought me a covered plate of fried chicken, and still no Kate. Men watched the street and ate what would be the last supper for some of them. I had coffee going on the stove and ate the chicken while it boiled. The night wind was blowing outside and I felt cold even with the stove going. I heard one of the Flannery boys coming in to report to his father, who was down at the hotel. After that it was quiet.

McLandress knocked and came in with a flushed face

and an awkward look on it. The old fool had changed his black banker's clothes for his militia uniform of yester-year. Needless to say, it didn't fit him, far too tight across the belly and hips. I guess he couldn't find the militia hat, because he still wore his banker's tile square on the middle of his head, as always.

We nodded and I wondered what he was up to. I knew it had nothing to do with Ballard. I pushed the bottle his way, but he submitted that black coffee would be better, after all. When there were cups of coffee steaming for both of us, he decided to dollop in a taste of whiskey, and I did the same. Only then did he start to inch his way toward the point of this get-together.

He started off by saying he was sorry we'd started out with bad feeling. I mumbled something appropriate and busied myself with coffee. McLandress took a long swig from his whiskey-laced java.

"You've been doing a fine job," he said. "Organizing the defenses and so forth. You know how it's done and you're doing it. If we succeed it will all be due to you."

I had $14 in my pocket, he knew how thin my roll was, so it couldn't be money. He had no way of knowing about the cash and jewels I hoped to get from Kate. And he was too friendly, however awkward, to be leading up to the money his daughter planned to lift from his bank. Which reminded me—where the hell was Laurie?

"No false modesty, sir," McLandress protested though I hadn't said a word. "When you first came to this town I didn't like you. Not so much you personally, but what I thought you were. Well, I was wrong, and I'm man enough to admit it."

I like a man who thinks he's so wonderful he can be humble. "What's done is done," I said amiably.

"You're made of the right stuff, I can see that now," McLandress said. "You've battered around a lot. Wild oats, sir. A man is all the better when he gets that out of his system."

I didn't like the way he talked about my oats in the past

tense. My firm intention was to sow a lot more before I got killed.

"A man with your character and resolution could be somebody in no time at all." McLandress took another belt of coffee and that put more fire in his face. "It isn't what a man has been but what he is now, if you follow my meaning. Of course you do." Then he gave it to me with both barrels. "My little girl Laurie is mighty fond of you."

It wasn't a joke because McLandress wasn't a joker. Humor was as foreign to him as a Chinaman would be to an Apache.

"A fine young lady," I said gallantly. "A credit to you and your lovely wife."

McLandress dismissed his lovely wife with a grunt. "About my daughter, yes and no," he said. "May I be frank, sir. How shall I put it? Laurie, though you'd never know it to look at her, is a little on the wild side. Heavens, I don't know where she got it from. Of course I have done a few wild things in my time. Haven't we all, sir?"

"A few wild oats," was the best I could come up with.

"Exactly," McLandress said. "Still, my little girl is a bit wild. When I say that I naturally don't mean—"

"Of course not," I said.

"I knew you'd understand. The fact is, she was always on the wild side. I thought that school in Charleston—cost me a pretty penny—would make her more settled. However, she returned with the same restless spirit. To come to the point, sir, I think she needs a husband."

"He's going to be a lucky man, whoever he is," I said with that gallows feeling that always comes over me, chilling my blood, when I'm threatened with matrimony.

"Not just any man, Mr. Saddler. Is it all right if I call you Jim?"

"That's my name . . . Dougal."

"The right man is what she needs, son. Laurie's had her pick of some fine men, most of them very well fixed, but none of them suit her. All she says is, 'Oh fudge!' when I bring some young man to the house for dinner. A young man, well not exactly young, came all the way from St. Louis, and she caused me great embarrassment by laughing at him."

"High spirits," I suggested.

"Exactly, son. Laurie says bankers and businessmen can go fly a kite, words to that effect. I think what she needs is a man who can tame her, if you know what I mean."

I did but I didn't say it because I didn't want to get into a gunfight with a banker. He didn't know what Laurie needed and neither did I. Laurie didn't. She knew what she liked but what you like isn't always what you need. His lovely little girl was hot as a pistol and no lone man would ever be enough to cool her down. Me, I didn't think she'd ever cool down; the fire between her thighs would never go out. I liked the thought and she would too, if she had known about it. Why shouldn't she stay randy as long as she had the will to spread her legs? I didn't say any of that to Dougal McLandress.

"Will you marry her?" McLandress held up his hand to stop me from talking. "I know this is sudden, but I'm convinced that you're the right man for her. There are differences in background, well yes, there's that, but nothing that can't be ironed out. Laurie hasn't any money of her own"—McLandress bore down heavily on this point—"and I am far from a wealthy man, no matter what you have heard about bankers. However, I have a modest store of worldly goods and am prepared to help my little girl's husband in every way I can."

"I'd be a washout at the banking business," I said.

McLandress looked startled as if he hadn't considered letting me get close to the real money. He trusted me enough to marry his daughter, but not to marry his money.

"To each his own," McLandress said, glossing over any talk of banking. "The cattle business, that's where you belong, son. Not a very large ranch, not at first anyway. Unfortunately, there isn't the money for that. But with a good woman at your side and plenty of hard work, you'd be a man of substance in no time. I won't press you for an answer, scarcely the time, is it, but I want you to think about it. Think of it, son, McLandress and Saddler, ranchers."

I thought about it after he took his rifle and went out. I didn't like it and Laurie wouldn't either. Not for me, the long back-breaking days in the saddle, the brain-boiling summers and ass-numbing winters. Worse than anything, I'd have Dougal McLandress both as partner and father-in-law. If we came through the fight with Ballard, the banker's whiskey-fired recklessness wouldn't last long. In a day or two, he'd be back to what he was, a smalltown banker. I knew Laurie would giggle when I told her, if I got to tell her, for only a dullhead like McLandress could see Laurie cooking and washing and mending, getting up in the dark to cook breakfast, falling wearily into bed after the last chores of the endless day were done. There wouldn't be much time, or energy, for Laurie to do the kind of things she liked to do in bed. I was thinking how crazy the whole thing was when there was another knock at the door. Whoever knocked had a light touch and I figured it was Kate. It wasn't, it was her father, standing in the doorway not like the wrath of God but like any other mortal. I waved him in and he asked if he could have a drink.

I gave it to him. "Nothing yet?"

"No sign of them. My boy Emmet just reported in. My brother and the other two are waiting out there on the road. They've been staring at that busted wagon wheel since it got dark." He turned the whiskey glass in his fingers, then without warning he said it.

"You've had to do with my girl, haven't you?"

I didn't answer and he went on without waiting for one. "I know you have. It's been in her face."

I said, "What do you want, Flannery?"

"Cool off," he said. "I'm not hot about it, why should you be? Men and women get together, it's the way of life. You like her or not?"

"I like her a lot."

"That's what I was afraid of."

"If I wanted to marry her I wouldn't ask you."

"Then you aren't going to marry her. You plan to go off with her?"

"If it's any of your business—no!"

Flannery drank the whiskey he'd been staring at. "That's good news . . . for you."

I needed the drink I poured. I was beginning to wish Ballard and his pistoleros would show up. "Meaning you'd try to kill me if I said yes?"

Flannery didn't rush in with an answer, but when it came I knew he meant it. "I'd just feel sorry for you," he said. "You'd be in plenty of trouble if you got tangled up tight with my Katie. You think it's funny, a father talking like this?"

"Not funny," I said. It was taking a turn I hadn't expected and didn't like.

"Call it odd then," Flannery said, filling our glasses. "Katie's a wild woman and she'll bring you down, if you let her. Other girls are wild and get over it. That won't happen with Katie. I don't say she's bad. There's something missing in her, that's all. I knew it all the time she was growing up. That's what all the fighting was about. Katie's trouble is she doesn't know what she wants. She says she does but she doesn't. I been sitting out there in the dark thinking about her, about you, this town."

"You came to it late," I said. "What difference does it make now?"

"Not much. But when I look at the townspeople out there it makes me feel bad. I had them figured for sheep, thought they didn't matter. Some of them are going to get killed because of my girl. I shouldn't have let it get this far. I should have forced her to go north with the boys along to protect her."

"That wouldn't be much better than Danziger. All along I've been telling people she isn't a runaway slave. Now I'm telling you. If she wants to stay in Dragoon Wells, that's what she should be able to do."

Gunfire erupted in the distance and we were on our feet and Kate Flannery was forgotten. It kept up as we ran to our positions and was still going on when we got there. The shooting stopped and then there was another quick spatter of shots. Nothing else after that. Our fire would be concentrated in two places, on both sides of the spike filled ditches, and at the only way out of town, the way they would come in. I looked down the street from a store window with all the glass knocked out, the resting place for the rifles clear of the jagged edges. The street was dark, with only a light showing here and there, but once the coal oil in the two separate ditches went off, there would be plenty of light to kill by.

Lights started to burn in some of the houses; that was the plan, to make it look like an alarmed town. Flannery and about half his men were across the street in the hotel; men were on the roofs on both sides. Outside of town horse hoofs thundered on the road. I began to count, knowing that one shot fired too soon would mean the end of us. Ballard's mind would jump to a trap; he would split his force and attack from four sides. I had made no provision for anything but an ambush; everything we had done depended on that.

The thunder of horses grew louder and on the night wind came the *yip-yip* cry of the Mexicans wanting to kill, loving the thought of killing. It sounded like an army was bearing down on us. I had been in plenty of fights, but you never get used to that sound. The thunder of the hoofs grew hollow for a moment; they were passing over the bridge that spanned the creek on the south edge of town. In a minute.

Then I saw the flare of their firebrands as they swept into the main street like a black flood. Seventy-five, hell! It was more like 100 Mexicans down there, and they came on like a force that couldn't be stopped. The howl of their bloodlust, their ancient hatred of gringos, filled the flame smudged night. A cold wind blew but there was sweat on my face as I steadied the Winchester and waited for them to get closer. I kept looking for Ballard in that first wild rush of men and horses, trying to pick him out from the oncoming torrent of noise and big hats and rifles.

They hit the first ditch at breakneck speed and men and horses plunged to their deaths in a welter of flapping wagon covers and gunshots and screams. I cut loose at the same time as Flannery across the street. Heavy fire broke out at the far end of the street. McLandress and the townspeople were driving them forward toward the death-filled ditches. Twenty-five or 30 horses and men were brought down by the first ditch, and those behind, driven forward by their own numbers and speed, piled in after them. Some jumped the first ditch and then hit the second. The coal oil beyond the third ditch licked up bright yellow and the flames were fanned higher by the wind. Some got across the first and second ditches by riding over the mass of dead and dying flesh. Not so many dead or dying Mexicans were tangled in the last ditch. No horse could get out of there, but men were crawling up the steep sides.

Then nine or ten Flannerys rose up from behind the wall of fire and drove them back, firing like infantrymen, down on one knee, levering and firing. From end to end the street was a screaming mass; rifles and handguns spat orange fire. A shotgun boomed one barrel, then the other. I killed five men with five shots and grabbed up another rifle when the pin clicked on empty. It was impossible to tell one attacker from another.

Now they were trying to turn, firing back as they rounded their horses short of the first ditch. They were still crawling out of the ditches, and I fired until the shots ran together, and still they came. I fired at a big man in a big hat and killed him, but he died yelling Spanish and I knew he wasn't Ballard. They were very good, the way they rallied. The wall of fire was weakening and the Flannerys moved through it firing as they came. The Mexicans rounded on them and cut a swath through their ranks with a heavy burst of fire.

At that point the Mexicans had a chance of breaking loose, but instead of going over the last ditch they turned back again, taking their losses, trying to overcome us with firepower. As they turned and came back, many on foot now, they poured lead at our positions. Bullets chipped stone close to my face.

A horseman galloped straight at the window I was firing from. I killed him and then the horse and the weight of their charge tore the window frame loose from the wood, and for a moment I was blinded by dust. I wiped dirt from my eyes and started firing again. Now they were trying to get out through the alleys and open spaces, and I heard them screaming in the dark as they galloped into the wire. The street was piled high with bodies, shapes, things still moving. A man was trapped under a horse, still firing with a pistol though his legs were shattered. I shot him in the head and the horse that pinned him jumped up and ran a few steps before it dropped again and died.

At the other window two men fell back and one was shot in the face and blinded and ran at the wall. The other man was dead. I grabbed the two rifles and moved out onto the sidewalk. A man running behind me was hit and fell down. He grabbed his leg and hauled himself up by holding onto a porch support. A bullet killed him as he swayed.

Across the street the Flannerys were coming from the hotel and on the roofs men were crawling their way closer to the alleys. A Mexican ripped by wire and slick with blood ran from the dark and was shot to bits. Two Flannerys dropped and then a third and I heard Con Flannery cursing the others forward into the fight. McLandress and the others were moving up from the south end to close the trap, and the men on the roofs gave them cover as they came.

The last of the Mexicans, maybe 20, bunched up and were torn apart by fire until they reformed and tried to break out through the south end of the street. I yelled at Flannery and he turned, rallying his men, and now we had the last of the Mexicans between us. We opened fire as they charged at McLandress's town men. We closed in on them still firing, and when the guns were empty we pulled them down and beat and kicked and stomped them to death. Then with one last yell of defiance some of them broke through the mass of men and ran into the open chased by bullets.

Con Flannery looked at me, mad eyed with the joy of killing, and ran with his men following, through the hotel and out to the back where their horses were saddled and waiting. I heard them riding away as the rest of us got on with the killing.

I dropped my empty rifle and yanked my beltgun when Peyton Ballard rose up in front of me, the big Mexican hat cinched tight under his chin and hiding his face. He was wounded in the chest and holding a gun and was trying to bring it up to shoot. He fired and missed and the hammer came back under my thumb but I didn't fire. I dived at his legs and brought him down, and even with the wound he fought like a tiger. I still held the gun and I hammered at his skull until he went limp and I forced myself to stop. It was McLandress, smelling strongly of whiskey, of all people, who pulled me away from Ballard. I was smeared with Ballard's blood and I stood weak on rubber legs. McLandress got down beside the body and said it wasn't a body.

"He's alive, we can hang him," he said, turning his big white face to me.

Then I reloaded both rifles and we moved in after the last of the Mexicans, and they were game greasers and they all died well. Shooting broke out in an alley and a townsman, killed by a Mexican, bled to death with a strand of wire dug into his throat.

McLandress, full of whiskey, was a wild man. Men who get a taste of killing grow to like it. "Some are still alive," he said, shaking with excitement. "We'll hang them too."

"Just shoot them," I said. "Only Ballard hangs."

And that's what we did, where we found them, and I had to keep some of the townsmen, the tame clerks and storekeepers, from killing them slow. It was no quick job: they were all over the place, mostly wounded. Men lit firebrands and the killing went on. We flushed them out, dragged them out, and killed them. Not a single man tried to give up—they were Mexicans! There was so much killing, and it had to be done. Shooting sounded from far away and I knew the Flannerys had caught up with the survivors, not all of them, of course, just most of them. A few would get away, and they would be hunted through the hours of darkness and long after daylight came. Even so, a handful would survive to carry the bloody story back to Sonora. I killed a man crawling under a sidewalk and then I stopped. I was sick of killing. Let the townsmen have their fun; after all, it was their town and their big night.

They killed the last Mexican when the sky was red with the coming day. The funny thing was he didn't have a mark on him; stunned by a fall from his horse, he had been out cold through the whole thing. Now he stood up on shaky legs and looked about in wonder at the bodies still being dragged and piled high for burial. Light was in the street and everything washed in red when he got up. He picked up his hat and his hand went down to his empty holster. He was young and his smile was apologetic and yet mocking. McLandress looked to me for guidance, no longer eager to kill, now that he had to do it in the full light of day. I nodded and Bush the stable man shot the boy from behind.

It was all over but the hanging.

FIFTEEN

We *didn't wait for the Flannerys to get back—we just* did it. Ballard wasn't like Danziger; he didn't say a word. No bribes were offered and no defense. It would have been useless, so he didn't try. Ballard looked older than his age, hollow eyed as if from no sleep or bad sleep, and as we walked him down to the livery stable he didn't ask about Kate. Where was Kate? Seven members of her family were dead, one as good as, and there wasn't a sign of her. Two women had been killed, but Kate wasn't one of them. I guessed she could wait.

We had the rope ready to be slung from the hay hoist when old Dad Switzer came limping into town, ragged and bloody but otherwise all right. The crowd assembled to see Ballard hanged gave way to let the old man through. He spat when he saw Ballard. He didn't say anything about the men who had been with him on the road. I knew they were dead, cut down in the first few minutes.

"Is this the great man?" the old man asked.

"This is him," I said.

Dad Switzer said he would take it as a great favor if he could hang this one. "I won't have to trip this one," he said.

He didn't. Dad and McLandress and Bush took Ballard up and he stepped out the window by himself. I don't know what I expected from Ballard, but I didn't get it. Nothing marked him for the notorious outlaw he had been. The years seemed to have worn him down; he didn't look like a well man, and it wasn't just the battle that had taken the life out of him. Liquor and sickness and age had done most of it; darlin' Kate had done the rest. And where in hell was that beautiful bitch?

They put Ballard's body with his Mexicans; he came last so he got the top spot. There was an argument about whether they should bury them in the cemetery. It didn't last long and they buried them in the cemetery, all in one big pit it took hours to dig. It didn't look deep enough to me, and I suggested that they dump in all the lime they could find. McLandress, sick-looking now, said that was a highly practical idea.

Con Flannery came back while we were standing over the graves of our own people. We hadn't buried any of the Flannerys; where they got planted was for Con to decide. He walked up and down the row of dead faces; two had been his brothers, men who had made the long haul with him. Con Flannery looked at them and that was all.

"Bury them with their friends," he said.

And then we straggled back to town. Our losses had been heavy enough, 19 men and two women; and as the townspeople walked back I saw that early grief was now replaced with quiet pride. They had done the impossible, all these ranchers and storekeepers. Old Dr. Kline had died of the excitement. It was a hell of a thing. Kate the beautiful bitch—where was Kate? She was free now, could go where she pleased and not have to think of Ballard. So many men had died because of her. Strictly speaking, that wasn't true, yet men were dead. I had kept the faith with her, and now I wanted to be gone. Callahan and his Goddamned job didn't press too heavy on my mind. Besides, something bigger than a mildly crooked marshal's broken legs had happened in Dragoon Wells, and they wouldn't think much about Callahan for a while. Truthfully I was past caring what happened to Johnny; life was a prizefight and he would have to duck the punches or go under.

Some of the community spirit had worn off by the time the sun was hot in the sky. Everything passes, good fellowship quicker than anything else. Men stood staring at their shattered windows and bullet-broken furniture. Already there was squabbling about how the ditches were to be filled in and the street put back the way it was. A man complained that he didn't live at the end of town where the ditches were, the ditches that had saved his life. Casey was dead and I had been surprised to hear that. I had figured he would dodge out the back way. They say you should never get to know too much about a man you despise. Do that and you'll be forced to change your opinion. Maybe so.

Let them squabble. I was through with Dragoon Wells. All I wanted was a lot of liquor before I quit the town for good. But first—Kate. I would look for her when I had a drink, two drinks, probably more. I took off my badge and put in on the desk. Then I got sick of looking at it and threw it in a drawer. A little later I heard noise and went out to see what it was.

It was Kate—and Callahan! Kate was driving the fancy black-and-gold-trimmed buggy, and Callahan sat beside her like a fool, still in splints but livelier than the last time I'd seen him. Kate reined in the horse, but they didn't climb down. Con Flannery looked up from shoveling dirt, and that's all he did.

I went over. "You should have been here last night," I told Callahan. I was feeling mean.

"I'm getting out," Callahan said, shoving a roll of

money at me. I put it in my pocket without looking at it. "The job's all yours if you want it," Callahan said. "Kate and me are going up north."

I looked at Kate, so mean and beautiful. She was wearing the same green dress she came in.

"Congratulations," I said. Callahan didn't know what he was getting into. Or maybe he did, and didn't care. If he had lost his nerve, like Casey said, he had it back. Those two, Callahan and Kate, went back a long way, and there were things between them there was no knowing about. Could be they were wrong enough to be right together. Callahan hadn't always been a smalltown crook, and maybe a man still lived behind the dandy front. I didn't understand the man anymore than I understood Kate. Kate, I don't know how I felt about her. It was too late to ask her about the money. I couldn't and I wouldn't. Like the man said, I'd been had.

"Why don't you keep the job?" Johnny said, wanting to get out from under everybody's stares. No one came close, not even McLandress. Kate remained silent. "They never liked me," Johnny said. "After what you did, you won't have any trouble. Why didn't you let me know what was going on?"

"You couldn't have helped," I said. "Not your fault. I was busy." I looked around at the town I hoped I would never see again. "The town is better off without you— and me. They'll find a good man, they always do."

Callahan didn't say where they were going; up north was a big place. "We'd better be on our way," he said without offering to shake hands.

Kate spoke for the first time. "There's something in the desk drawer, Saddler. I left it there this morning. Goodbye, Saddler. Try not to get killed. There's only one of you"—she smiled a real smile—"and maybe that's a good thing."

Kate shook the reins and clicked her tongue and the buggy moved on. She didn't look at her father as they passed him. Flannery looked after her and went back to digging. The buggy went away and I never saw Kate again.

In the desk drawer I found the money she had promised. No jewelry, just bright Mexican gold pieces. The count was exactly right. The beautiful bitch had kept her word and I was a rich man while it lasted. I didn't feel bad about Kate. We had what we had and it was over. There was a note written in a strong bold hand with a forward slant. I grinned. Even her handwriting was tough, brassy, independent.

Dear Saddler:

You're too much man for me, so here's your money and good-bye. I'm going to think about you, you arrogant son of a bitch. But I have to find something safer than you. Grin all you like, turdhead, I'm going to try. If I fail, then fuck it. I'd have no chance at all if I stayed with you. You're bad and I'm worse, so you see it's hopeless. I'm going back to Johnny to see if he will have me. I will have a better chance with him. At least he's not crazy.

Kate

I was putting the money in my saddlebag when McLandress bustled in. The fat man was on his way back to being a banker. I knew there was going to be more talk about his daughter; it was far from what I expected to hear. My, he was all worked up.

"I want you to arrest my daughter," he said.

You can believe my jaw dropped when I heard that. "You know what you're saying?"

McLandress sat down heavily but shook his head at my whiskey. "Not arrest exactly," he said, a man much troubled. "Seeing that we have a sort of understanding about Laurie I can be frank with you. However, what I'm going to say must not get beyond this room."

"Never," I said.

McLandress nodded. "Laurie tried to rob the bank early this morning. My wife followed her and caught her opening the safe. She had an empty carpetbag, her intention was plain. My wife is watching her right now. She had to lock her in her room."

"You want me to have a talk with her?" I said sternly. "Make her realize the terrible disgrace she nearly brought on the family?"

McLandress was more banker than father. "Stronger than that," he said. "Threaten to send her to jail if she doesn't behave. As a matter of fact, son, this is a good time to start telling her what to do. As her future husband, that is." McLandress knew he was laying it on too thick, so he softened a little. "At heart she's a good girl, but he needs a firm hand."

"She'll get it," I said. "I'll go and talk to her right now."

"Good boy!" McLandress said. "Don't go easy on her, son. Bear down hard on her."

"You bet I will . . . Dad." I couldn't wait to bear down on lovely Laurie. She was a criminal, and I was going to tell her that the minute I got her into bed.

On the way to the house, McLandress said the joyriding was over for Laurie. From now on there would be nothing but solid good sense, plenty of hard work. After the wedding both of us would keep an eye on her to see she didn't stray into the pathways of sin and all the other things that make life worth living.

McLandress clapped me on the shoulder as we went into the house. "I'm never wrong about a man once I make my final decision," he said. "You're all right, son. Go on up now. Room's at the end of the hall. Mrs. McLandress and I will wait down here."

"It's best you don't come up," I agreed. Mrs. McLandress gave me a motherly smile that chilled my soul.

I knocked before I turned the key in the lock and went

in, and there she was sulking by the window. God! she was such a hot-crotch beauty, and still quivering with anger.

"You're a bad girl," I said with a straight face.

"Fuck you—you're the one that fucked it up! Why the hell didn't you come with me? Now I don't have a cent and never will. And what's this shit my father keeps talking about? You and me married, in the cattle business. You double-crossed me, Saddler. Let me down. If you think I'm going to live on some shitty little ranch, you know what you can do."

I grinned at her. "It's a good clean wholesome life," I said. "Working hard, raising lots of kids, watching them grow. Church on Sunday, box lunches in the afternoon. Forget about going to Mexico City, living in posh hotels, spending money in fancy stores, dining in big restaurants. You'll forget all that the minute we're married and have our own little ranch."

I think Laurie had been measuring the drop from the window when I came in. "I'd rather die," she said. "That's what I'll do—I'll drink poison. You'll be sorry when I'm dead, you big bastard!"

It wasn't the time or place, but I reached for her, and we grabbed at each other before we tumbled into her pretty canopied bed.

"Shush!" I warned her.

I reached for her and she pushed my hand away as if we were really married. "Oh, no," she said. "It was different the other time. You know I have no money, all you want is a quick poke."

"Well, it has to be quick, this time it has to," I said. "It's going to be hard, I'll just have to take you as you are. A poor penniless girl."

"Since when did you get so rich?"

"Since a minute ago."

Laurie let me do a few things under her dress. "You swear you aren't saying that just to get into my bloomers. That would not be the act of a gentleman. Go on— swear!"

I swore and then we made love and you'd never think there were two outraged parents waiting at the bottom of the stairs. When we finished Laurie snuggled up to me, still holding onto my cock.

"Don't get tired of me too soon, Saddler. It's all right when you do—I'll be all right—but don't do it too soon."

"The same goes for you," I said. "Of course you'll be all right. How could you help not be? You'll always be all right."

"I don't know that I like the way you say that."

"A compliment."

It was a compliment. No matter what happened Laurie would be all right. In the years to come, after I was gone and half forgotten, she would tumble out of a lot of beds. But she would always land on her feet. We would be good together, and we both knew it. I would do right by her in my own way; no harm would come to her and when it came time to break up, as it had to, I would see that she wasn't lacking for anything. The money from Kate would last a long time, even the way we'd spend it, and there would be more when that was gone. The world was full of money if you knew how to get at it. Laurie and I were friends, something I could never be with Kate; there's nothing better than getting into bed with a woman who is also a good friend.

"Now listen," I said when we had our clothes on and the bed was tidy again. "We can't go now or your folks will make a fuss. I won't go through that, even for you. Get packed but hide your bags until it's time to leave."

"Yes, sir," Laurie said, rubbing my yard through my pants. "When will that be?"

"As soon as it gets dark. I'll bring the horses around and you be ready when I do. How does Mexico City suit you? It's good to go somewhere without being chased."

Laurie smiled. "I want you to chase me a lot."

SADDLER

The hardest-riding, hardest loving cowboy who ever blazed a trail or set a heart on fire.

#1: A DIRTY WAY TO DIE by Gene Curry. When Saddler went to new Orleans for a good time with the ladies, he ended up accused of beating an old woman to death. He could have run, but if he didn't prove himself innocent his life would be worthless.
__2699-9 $2.95 US / $3.50 CAN

WILDCAT WOMAN by Gene Curry. Hired by a millionaire to find his spoiled daughter, Saddler knew the job was going to be tough. Soon the daughter's outlaw boyfriend was hot to put Saddler six feet under, and the wildcat heiress was even hotter to gun him down — between the sheets or anywhere else.
__2988-X $2.95 US / $3.50 CAN